Sparks fly when a small-town dairy farmer meets a big-city judge. Jake Coltrane seems too good to be true: an old-fashioned gentleman in faded jeans, with just the right mix of downhome wit, common sense, and timeless gallantry. Atlanta municipal court judge Vivian Costas is a streetwise urban gal who doesn't trust people in general and men in particular. But when this charming good ol' boy rescues her from a pair of thugs, then quickly sets out to win her heart, Vivian realizes that when it comes to falling in love recklessly, it's all right to be Just A Little Bit Guilty. Originally published as 'Cupid's Verdict' 1987, Berkley Books, New York.

Other BelleBooks Titles By Deborah Smith

Alice at Heart
Diary of a Radical Mermaid
The Crossroads Cafe
A Gentle Rain
Soul Catcher
Solomon's Seal

Coming Soon from Deborah Smith and BelleBooks

Clementine and Morning Glory
Kitchen Charms

Just a Little Bit Guilty

by

Deborah Smith

Bell Bridge Books

This is a work of fiction. Names, characters, places and incidents either are the products of the author's imagination or are used fictitiously. Any resemblance to actual persons (living or dead,) events or locations is entirely coincidental.

Bell Bridge Books
PO BOX 30921
Memphis, TN 38130
ISBN: 978-0-9843256-4-1

Bell Bridge Books is an Imprint of BelleBooks, Inc.
Copyright © 2009 by Deborah Smith

Printed and bound in the United States of America.

A mass-market edition of this book was published by Berkley Books Second Chance at Love in 1986 as *Cupid's Verdict*

We at BelleBooks enjoy hearing from readers. You can contact us at the address above or at BelleBooks@BelleBooks.com

Visit our websites – www.BelleBooks.com and www.BellBridgeBooks.com.

10 9 8 7 6 5 4 3 2

Cover design: Debra Dixon
Interior design: Hank Smith
Photo credits: Kurhan | Fotolia.com
:Lk:01:

Chapter One

Whump.

The sound reached his ears in the frosty night air at the precise moment the elderly woman's lethal shoulder bag connected with his denim-clad upper thigh, barely missing a part of his anatomy he prized highly. He gasped as pain shot down his leg.

"You pack a wallop for a little old bag lady," Jake Coltrane complained in a deep drawl. "Darlin', I'm only tryin' to help you."

She stumbled on the icy Atlanta sidewalk, obviously dazed, but kept swinging. Jake held his shotgun out of her arm's flailing arc and tried to close in for a grip on her. Under his heavy flannel shirt, his shoulder also ached fiercely from his encounter with whatever was heavy and sharp-edged inside her faded cloth shoulder bag.

"Ma'am, I'm not one of the muggers. They've run off. I've got half a mind to run off myself, if you whack me again."

"Get back, ass wipe," she mumbled, rabbit punching the air with one fist.

For an old lady, she had a mouth on her. *She looks like a fuzzed-up Bantam hen in all those scarves and coats.* He circled her, pawing at her gently. He nearly stumbled over the two blue tick hounds who hung on his heels, growling.

"Hush, Chester. Hush, Phoebe. Chester, get out of my way. Granny's gettin' more addled by the second."

The tiny bag lady made a low, squealing sound of

defiance and swung again. Jake dodged the blow. She hissed. "Back off, I've got a Taser," she said. She staggered. The run-down heels on her ancient leather shoes slipped on the ice, and she sat down hard on the crumbling cement. Her ankle-length coat top coat flew up. In the stark glow of a security light Jake caught a glimpse of slender black leggings on curvaceous legs above furry white ski boots. He frowned. How many homeless old women looked like back-up singers for Bjork under their coats? And how many bag ladies had a swing like a bouncer at a rave? She scrambled to her feet again, slapping at the hand he extended and weaving back and forth unsteadily.

"Ma'am," he persisted. "I know you've been knocked in the head and you're scared pretty bad, but just quit swingin' at me. I'm not trying to punk you or rob you or . . . or whatever. I came out here to chase those dudes off and help you."

All he could see of her face was a pair of lustrous dark eyes. They gazed woozily at him from below a purple-felt skull cap. Her lower face was hidden behind a lime-green scarf wrapped several times around her head. She blinked slowly then stopped like a wobbling Weeble, her knees bumping each other, the weight of her heavy bag throwing her off-balance. She weakly lifted one gloved hand and pointed at him with menace as he inched forward.

"You . . . better be . . . for real," she murmured thickly, an instant before she fainted across his outstretched arms.

She was at least a foot shorter than him, and more bulky than heavy. Jake carried her easily to his battered red pickup truck, parked just a few feet away on the oak-lined street, and deposited her on the passenger side. She moaned and rested her head on the truck's cold vinyl seat. With gentle, work-scarred fingers, Jake tried to pull the scarf away from her face and unbutton her coat, but she pawed his hand away.

"Keep your groping little . . . groping little mitts to yourself, mister," she warned, her voice muffled and her eyes groggy. "You may be . . . may be huge . . . but if you think I won't try to Taser you right in the . . . "

"Darlin', I'm not goin' to hurt you," he assured her. "I'm gonna drive you over to Grady's ER, okay? You stay quiet while I put my dogs up and get my coat. Be right back."

He shook a finger at her, but her eyes had already closed. Jake took the opportunity to look closely, bending forward. He sniffed tentatively. Her clothes smelled musty, but he also noted a scent of light, expensive perfume. Huh. Probably a knock-off store brand she stole off some street vendor.

He frowned harder. What he could see of her face above the scarf had no distinct age lines. And she had the thickest, blackest lashes.

Those inky lashes fluttered up, revealing pain and fear and confusion. "What's your name, douche bag?"

Jake patted her bulky, shapeless lap, hoping he was hitting some neutral area, like a knee. She must have a mild concussion. "I'm Jake Coltrane. I own that run-down old apartment building we were in front of."

She blinked. "*Where* am I?"

A thread of true anxiety weaved its way into Jake's mind. She must be hurt worse than he'd thought. He patted her leg or lap or whatever was under her layers of dingy clothes. "You're with me, darlin'. And that means you're safe."

"Not likely," she whispered. But her eyes shut

again.

Jake rushed his dogs inside the apartment building, locked them in his rooms, then raced back outside. His bag lady still sat with her eyes shut, unmoving.

He drove like hell, punching nine-one-one on his cell phone as he drove.

The trip to Atlanta's Grady Memorial Hospital took only fifteen minutes through the shadowy city streets, since it was near midnight on a weekday. During the ride, the bag lady huddled in the far corner of the passenger side, her eyes shut and her arms crossed over her dirty beige coat.

"What's *your* name?" Jake asked as he swung the truck next to the curb across from Grady's emergency entrance. He switched off the ignition and flipped his tractor cap onto the dash. "I'll need to tell them inside. Here they come, darlin'. They're bringing a stretcher for you."

All he received for his trouble was a pained grunt, so he gingerly reached over and opened her floppy bag. It had fallen onto the floor next to the stick shift.

"Let's see if I can find something with your name on it . . . good Lord!"

The weapon that had nearly poked a hole in him twice was a thick volume of the Georgia Criminal Code. Jake pulled it out slowly and whistled under his breath. Where this little old character had gotten it, he couldn't imagine. Maybe she'd robbed a lawyer.

She wavered upright and tried to shove his hands away from her bag. "That's personal."

"Easy darlin', easy," Jake replied. He wrapped one broad-knuckled hand gently around both of her wrists and held her captive while he continued to delve into her belongings. "I've got to find some ID for you."

But all he found was a dollar in change and a new-looking set of Prius keys on a key ring. He stared at the keys with his mouth open. She slumped limply against the door, her eyes shut tight in pain. "Don't feel . . . so . . . good, Jake," she mumbled. "Nauseated."

He went into immediate action, climbing out of the truck and running to the passenger side. She shoved her door open and rolled out before he could reach her. Her feet hit pavement that was slick with the oil and gas stains of the orange-striped ambulances that parked there regularly. She slid and he grabbed her, swinging her up into his arms as if she were a child. Her head rolled against his shoulder.

"Put me down, Tarzan," she croaked. "I'm Vivian, not Jane."

"So it's Vivian," he answered softly, kicking the door shut with the toe of his work boot. "Well, Vivian, you've got more spunk than a spring heifer. Let's get you to a doctor."

"Thank you," she whispered.

He worked his way between a row of ambulances and carried her through heavy double doors into a scene straight out of a Tim Burton movie version of hell. Police suspect with bloody faces were handcuffed to chairs against institutional-green walls. People moaned and screamed and cursed. Atlanta police officers nonchalantly guided drug dealers and hookers up the halls.

Jake paused inside the door, his face grim. He'd never seen anything like this at Doc Murtha's office in his Tennessee hometown. Not even on the Saturday night following the fall carnival.

"Whoo-whee!" a scrawny man called from one corner. "It's Jed Clampett! And Granny!"

Jake gave him a silencing glare. His big shoulders flexed under his sheepskin coat as he looked down into the bag lady's half-shut eyes, seeing them in bright light for the first time. He inhaled sharply. They were a hickory-nut hazel, sprinkled with gold and edged in black. Those amazing lashes of hers made shadows on the youthful, olive-hued skin of her cheeks. Her head tucked into the cradle of his shoulder, she blinked up at him slowly, blankly, like a wounded doe.

"What you got there, man?"

Jake lifted startled eyes to find a huge police officer with a head full of short, inky dreads. At six-two, Jake wasn't accustomed to tilting his head back to meet another man's gaze. His jaw tightened as he assessed the distrust and dislike in the policeman's eyes. "I'll hang with her, man."

The officer jerked his thumb toward and empty stretcher. "Leave her, and I'll get a doc."

"No." Jake couldn't leave this wistful, pugnacious little woman alone in this hell hole.

"I'll get you a younger bitch, if you're *that* desperate!" a greasy-faced blond with a swollen eye chided. A chorus of guffaws rose around Jake. Jake slowly clenched his fists.

The officer shook his head and sighed. "Cool off, man. Let's see what we got here. Ol' mama, come on now, lemme get an identity on you." He reached over, tugged the scarf down around Vivian's chin, and gently turned her face toward him.

His mouth popped open. "Judge Costa!" he exclaimed.

The officer pivoted and yelled across the admissions lobby. "Bill! It's the judge from municipal court! It's Vivian Costa."

"Why . . . Officer Washington, I didn't . . . know you cared," Vivian slurred.

"She's a what?" Jake echoed. "A judge?"

Jake stared down at her newly uncovered face, and his heart did a slow pirouette of surprise at what he saw. After a second of suspended animation, in which he absorbed every feature from the black wings of her brows to the firm little chin beneath her luscious, serious mouth, Jake understood perfectly why he had jelly behind his kneecaps.

She was adorable

Her face had a gentle, diamond shape. Her nose was short and slightly tilted, with a square, delicate tip. She had layered, feathery hair just long enough to brush the tops of her shoulders.

She was first prize at the livestock show.

附 • 附

Vivian was dimly aware of Jake Coltrane's arms tightening around her, and of his long, warm sigh brushing her face. He really did make her feel safe, now that she was over her initial shock at his assistance. In fact, she'd never felt so safe in her *life*. Her mental image of this man was dim, but his voice, the warm leathery scent of his coat, and his steady, gentlemanly grasp overwhelmed her with a sense of comfort.

"Y'all clear the way for Judge Costa!" the policeman thundered.

With the officer as a human battering ram, Jake carried his charge through more double doors. He hardly noticed when busy medical personnel glanced up from a forest of patients, examining tables, and equipment. Still staring down at Vivian Costa, his blood rushing too loudly inside his ear drums, he bumped his knee on a trash can and stopped distractedly. Jake glanced up to see a middle-aged, dark-skinned woman in jeans and a white lab coat bustling towards them, shaking her finger at Washington.

"Barney Washington, what do you think you're doing?" she interrogated with a Latin accent.

"Dr. Hernandez, it's Judge Costa!" the officer protested, looking hurt.

"It's Vivian? No!" Jake watched as the doctor grasped Vivian's hand. "Hey, Judge, you are causing some trouble again, eh?"

"Eh," Vivian agreed weakly. "Maria? Is that you?"

"Yeah, sure is. Make a joke so I know you're alive."

"He saved me, Maria. Do you believe that? A stranger . . . risked his hide . . . to save me." She paused, and a wistful smile curved her lips. "Isn't he unbelievable?"

"Yeah, really." Jake found the doctor's sharp eyes on him as her fingers gauged Vivian's pulse. "You. Mister. Who are you, and what has happened?"

"She was mugged outside my apartment building," Jake said patiently. He realized the he was grinning down at Vivian Costa so widely that his mouth hurt. Her compliment made him feel strong and needed, and at this point in his lonely life, he particularly appreciated that. "Two guys hit her in the head. She's all fainty and disoriented. Though she lands a pretty good punch and she still claims she's got a Taser on her, somewhere."

"Ah! Sounds like a concussion." Dr. Hernandez waved for him to follow her and started across the crowded examination room toward a gurney in one corner.

"Thanks, man, for bringin' her in," Barney Washington allowed. "She's our patron saint. She really cares about people."

"You!" Dr. Hernandez bellowed at Jake. "You, redneck! No more chatting. Come here."

With a nod to Officer Washington, Jake strode over. He carefully draped Vivian's small body on the padded table, while Dr. Hernandez arranged a curtain to afford a little privacy.

"You have strong arms, Jake Coltrane," Vivian whispered weakly. "Gentle arms."

"You're mighty easy to hold, ma'am," he told her, his breath shallow and hard in his throat. He'd have fought a whole army of muggers on her behalf. "You're just like a little sweet baby deer I once caught . . . "

She pressed a gloved hand to her forehead, and her mouth grimaced in distress. "Too many cornpone references . . . I . . . my head . . . please."

He slid his fingers under her sock cap and eased it off. Wavy hair the color and texture of chocolate-black silk flowed over his callused fingers as he massaged her scalp. She relaxed onto the gurney.

"Good," she sighed. "Makes the pain go away. Stay a . . . while."

"Easy, darlin', nobody could pry me outta here," he assured her gruffly.

He slipped his hand under her head and raised it for the pillow Dr. Hernandez placed underneath. Vivian turned her face into the antiseptic softness and sighed, her eyes closed again.

"Help or leave!" the doctor snapped.

Jake's big fingers fumbled at coats, scarves, and sweaters while the doctor ran practiced fingers over Vivian's scalp and peered into her eyes. Jake stopped, his stomach knotted, while the woman peeled her down to a University of Georgia sweatshirt and the black leggings.

You're a perfect little doll, Vivian Costa, Jake observed silently in continuing, breathless appreciation.

"Vivvy, you got a bump like Stone Mountain," Dr. Hernandez concluded, touching the right side of her head above one ear. "But your eyes aren't dilated, and you got some smarts, so I think we'll just order a couple of tests, watch you a while and let you go home. Are you still dizzy?"

"Only when I blink, dammit," Vivian mumbled. Jake took her hand and squeezed it. Vivian wanted to study him closely, to get a good look at this amazing man who showed such concern for her. But her head swam as she tried to focus, so she simply squeezed his huge hand back.

A nurse appeared with an ice bag, which Dr. Hernandez plopped into Jake's hand.

"Redneck, you sit here—" she pulled up a dirty, green stool, and he settled his big body onto it—"and hold this bag on her bump." She put her arms akimbo and eyed him warily. "You got that?"

He gave her an exasperated look. His sharp-edged drawl warned that he was tired of being the object of her sarcasm.

"I rescued her, ma'am. I got her here. I believe I can take care of the rest."

"Okay, okay." Dr. Hernandez's expression registered apology. "I'm sorry. Thanks." He smiled and shrugged. "Get her to talk more. Ask her things, and see if she makes sense."

With that, the doctor hurried off.

Like a man undertaking the most monumental duty of his life, Jake leaned over his ex-bag lady and followed the instructions Dr. Hernandez had just given.

ଓ • ଃଠ

The scent of a big, warm, male body close to her face invaded Vivian's nose and swam through her dull thoughts, zapping them into alertness. The ice bag brought welcome relief to the throb in her head and settled her churning stomach.

Maybe I am still human, she thought, here eyes closed. She tried to remember everything that had happened to her on the street, but couldn't. She could only picture the shotgun-toting man who kept calling her *darlin'* like some sort of NASCAR driver or country-western singer. He was the owner of the sandpaper-tipped fingers now stroking her temple. The pillow was cool and smooth on one side of her face; those fingers were hot and deliciously textured on the other.

The arm that occasionally brushed her cheek was covered in soft material that smelled good, earthy, and wood-smoked. Vivian sighed at the odd effect all those sensations had on her pulse rate, and turned her face toward the ceiling. Warm, masculine breath, pleasant and musky, filled her senses.

Her eyes opened clear and wide.

Whatever she'd expected paled next to the breathtaking reality of the welcoming, worshiping, magnetic blue gaze of the man who came into focus above her.

Chapter Two

"Batman," she managed finally, her heart racing. "Your bat costume is covered in flannel."

He smiled, then stopped smiling, then smiled again in slow, hypnotic sequence, widely and warmly, showing a glimpse of milk-white teeth between a stern upper lip and a generous lower one. His eyes—set in a handsome, open face with a blunt jaw—kept her spellbound.

The color of worn denim or clear sky on a summer day, those eyes never wavered. His ruddy, weathered complexion provided a contrasting backdrop, and stubby, thick eyelashes added brown accents. His brows and unruly hair were not quite red and not quite blond. His hair wanted desperately to curl, but because it was short on the sides and moderately long on top, the best it could manage was a glossy network of valleys and hills. He looked healthy and outdoorsy and sexier than any man had a right to be.

"You feelin' better, tough stuff?" he asked.

What a voice, she thought. "That's *Judge* Tough Stuff to you."

He chuckled and rearranged the ice bag gently. As her senses continued to sharpen, Vivian noticed a forest of reddish hair peeking over the collar of his blue plaid shirt.

"Thank you again for helping me," she murmured. Bits and pieces of the evening were beginning to creep back, but she still felt groggy. It was infinitely easier to think about him than to puzzle over her situation.

"You're sure welcome. Pleased to meet you. I never knew a judge could be so strong. Lord! Talk about the long arm of the law. I bet I've got bruises."

"I'm just a plain old first-arraignment judge," Vivian replied, smiling. "Just think how hard a superior court judge would have whacked you." Her smile faded. "But I'm really sorry."

"Forget about it. I thought all that swingin' and spittin' were cute."

He acted earnest and polite, sort of "Aw, shucks" and yet sophisticated in some way she couldn't define. Vivian wondered what in the world this sweet man was doing in the middle of her harsh, brash city. She wanted to protect him, and at the same time envied his fresh perspective. Vivian merrily twisted her Atlanta-bred lilt to mimic his heavy drawl.

"Well, Mr. Coltrane. What neck of the backwoods are you from?"

He leaned back, drew his heavy-soled work boots up so that his feet rested on the stool's bottom rung and gazed at her through narrowed eyes.

"I wouldn't make fun of you," he said quietly, with mild reproach. "And believe me, it'd be awful easy tonight."

After a long moment she nodded. "I'm sorry. I had a reason for dressing up and going out on the street." Vivian tried to cross her arms over her chest, but in the process her hands ran into the sheepskin covered brick wall of his arm. He still sat with that arm across her, holding the ice pack to her head. She snatched her hands down by her sides and felt her heart rate begin to sprint. She shifted self-consciously. "I was trying to get a look at the characters who've been robbing elderly women around the neighborhood."

"I'd say you got more than a look. Didn't anybody tell you that the judges do the sentencing and the police do the investigating?"

"Why, yes, Mr. Coltrane, I believe we covered that in Judge 101. Or maybe it was something I learned from an episode of *Law and Order*." She frowned at him fiercely, and a tendril of pain shot from the knot above her ear. "Ouch, dammit. You're pressing that ice pack too hard." She tried to move away from his disturbing touch.

"You got a smart mouth, girl. I gotta cool you off."

"You're asking for an assault charge, dude."

"It'd be worth it, Tough Stuff."

"Tough Stuff," she repeated sardonically. Her eyes shut as a wave of dizziness hit her. "If I'm tough it's because I have to be. *You* have to be, too. What you did tonight was crazy. Foolishly brave. I appreciate it—don't get me wrong—but I still don't understand why you cared enough to get involved." Now she could remember how cold the muggers' eyes had been. How dangerous. She still felt a hand grabbing at her throat.

"Why do people in the city act so suspicious?" Jake asked wearily. "Are you *all* this way? I couldn't let those men hurt you. Why is that so hard to figure?"

"Didn't it ever occur to you that you could have gotten hurt or killed . . . and all on behalf of a woman you don't even know?"

"They were hittin' you. They knocked you down." His voice was so angry toward the two men that Vivian felt tears spring to her eyes. He really cared. He was a rare soul. "When I think of what else they might have done . . . "

Nerves, fatigue and pain combined to make her tremble violently. Jake scrambled to his feet, and she opened her eyes as he put his coat over her.

"Hey, now, I'm real smart," he said dryly. "Scaring you, upsettin' you."

"Don't feel guilty. I scared myself."

She sighed gratefully and snuggled under his coat, twisting to lie on her side. He tucked it around her and sat back down. He put the ice pack in place again and let his hand rest on her shoulder. The contact was comforting, and she smiled up at him before closing her eyes drowsily.

"You can't go to sleep," he warned. "The doc said for me to ask you questions about yourself. You have to keep talking."

She squinted up at his somber face and rebelled at the confident baritone voice. "What kind of questions? I don't like to talk about myself."

"Why do you want to be so ornery?" Jake interjected, looking genuinely puzzled. "Why don't you act sweet like you were when you were addled?" Vivian blinked rapidly, astonished at how much his words stung. "I don't know how to be sweet, okay? There's no point in you hanging around, waiting to get insulted." He gazed down at her, surprise in his broad, handsome face. She ignored a twinge of self-rebuke. He made her feel embarrassed and mean and . . . oh, all right . . . ornery. Vivian avoided his blue eyes.

"Judge Costa," he said softly. He emphasized the 'Judge' as if he didn't care to be on a first-name basis with her anymore. His voice dripped insult. "If you don't know how to take help, then I feel sorry for you."

"Oh, don't take it so personally."

"You know," he continued, jabbing a blunt finger

at her, "I've been here in the city three months. My place has been robbed, kids stole the radio and the GPS out of my pickup, I got hookers pesterin' me for business and addicts askin' me for money I don't have. But I've acted friendly, and I've gotten a lot of friendliness in return."

He raised one red-gold brow at her. "Until I met you. You've got a streak of distrust in you a mile wide. Lord, I'd hate to have to throw myself on the mercy of *your* court."

He stood, towering over the examination table, and reached for his coat. Startled and more than a little ashamed, Vivian sat up quickly to blurt an apology. Maybe she'd seen too much ugliness to recognize the other extreme, she thought. Maybe she just couldn't bear to let him walk out of here. The ice pack slid off her head, and dizziness engulfed her. Realizing too late that moving fast had been a foolish thing to do, she pressed the heels of her hands to her temples and gasped. Immediately, his arms surrounded her.

"It's hard to be feisty when your bells are ringin', isn't it?" Jake taunted. But the anger had faded from his voice. Vivian raised yearning, wistful eyes to analyze him. His face was close to hers, his brow furrowed with concern, his mouth slanted down. She nodded limply. "Yeah, it's hard to be feisty." The room stopped moving, and she inhaled gratefully as he lowered her back to the gurney. Vivian held out one hand. Her eyes locked with his, she said contritely, "Mr. Coltrane, you have my sincere apology for being an ungrateful bee-atch."

For a moment, he continued to look upset then his face softened into a smile. The smile became wide, creasing his eyes at the corners sexily. He laughed low in his throat, and covered her little hand with his big one. Vivian's mouth went chalk-dry at the feel of is thick fingers pressing lightly into her palm. Jake gazed down at their joined hands, and his thumb caressed a blue vein under her delicate skin.

"Apology accepted, Tough Stuff." He cleared his throat. They weren't shaking hands, they were holding hands—without moving, without breathing. "I knew you really didn't want me to leave." He saw the shimmering wetness creep into here eyes before she could will it away. She turned her head toward the pillow.

"You poor, tired girl," he whispered, and touched her cheek. That did it. If he hadn't said those sappy, sweet words she could have held on, Vivian thought in despair, as a huge tear slide down the side of her nose. Jake's fingers brushed it away before she could stop him.

"It's . . . all . . . right," she assured him, her voice low and tight. "Forget it."
"Don't try to be such a tough little—"

"You're supposed to ask me questions, "she interjected abruptly, feeling absurd and ready not just to sniffle again but—as her hard-bitten mother, Julia, would have called it—to boo-hoo like a whiny loser. Why did this man make her feel this way? Her throat was graveled. "So, ask your questions! Ask!" she ordered.

She could feel him looking down at her sympathetically. She shrugged, sniffed, and turned her best courtroom poker face up to him. She watched dully, her head throbbing with new pain, as he pulled a spare tractor cap out of his back pocket. He studied it, fiddling with the adjustable band for a moment.

"What's your middle name?" he asked finally. He reached over and put the tractor cap on her head, cocking it to one side so it didn't touch her bump. Then he put the ice pack, which had slipped down the pillow, back in place.

"Fiona. Vivian Fiona Costa," she said slowly. Her mouth stayed open after the last part. His easy charm mesmerized her.

"That's pretty. I never knew an Italian girl before."

"My father's Italian. My mother's just your basic white-bread American."

He hung his heels on the stool's middle rung and propped his elbows on the white-blue denim that covered his knees. His hands hung casually between his legs. Vivian thought he had wonderful hands—mapped with scars and nicks and calluses, but as supple and caring as a surgeon's. "Your parents still alive, Tough Stuff?"

"Sort of. They moved to Pittsburg last year."

He chuckled. "What's your father do?"

"He sits around wishing he were back in Atlanta."

"What's he do for a livin', Ms. Wise Mouth?"

She couldn't help smiling at him. He smiled back.

"He's the best tailor in the world. He and my uncle Gino are partners in a men's clothing store. Custom suits. Old-world craftsmanship."

"You grew up in the middle of the city?" Jake looked around the noisy, smelly emergency room, distaste on his face. He seemed to feel that the scene around them summed up all that was wrong with city life.

"In a house about ten minutes from downtown," she told him tautly. "Midtown. Classic old bungalows. Big oak trees. Block parties." He looked unconvinced as his eyes studied her curiously. Vivian sighed. "So where are you from, Mr. Coltrane, beside that ancient apartment building on Crescent Street?"

"I'm from Tuna Creek, Tennessee," he said, exhaling and running one hand through his hair wearily. "Go ahead and laugh."

Vivian pushed his cap back with the edge of one thumb. *Don't laugh, don't laugh*, she ordered herself silently. She'd control herself with the same technique she used in court every time some gangbanger said something outrageous.

"Who named it Tuna Creek?" she asked sternly, as if she'd like to get her hands on the culprit.

"My great-granddaddy," he answered.

"Oh, crap."

But he started chuckling and shook his head to indicate there was no need for an apology. After a second, Vivian began to smile.

"Oh, oh, oh," she said, clasping her aching head. "This is torture."

"See, a travelin' salesman sold Great-Granddaddy some little bitty fish and told him they were a breed of freshwater tuna," Jake explained with fiendish pleasure, as she waved a hand to him to stoop. "And Great-Granddaddy dumped them in his creek."

"What were they?" she managed to sputter.

"Goldfish."

She laughed harder, holding her head.

"It worked out pretty well," Jake added somberly. "Except it was always hard to find enough plastic castles and colored rocks . . . "

"Stop!" she demanded, squinting in pain, her laughter fading. Immediately, he pulled the cap off her head and began stroking her temple. Vivian snuggled into the pillow and took deep breaths.

"You okay, Tough Stuff?"

She nodded. "How'd you end up living in Atlanta?" she wanted to know.

"I lost my dairy business to the bank," he said softly.

His fingers paused, and Vivian gazed up at him to find his face set in a stoical line but his attention suddenly miles away.

"Everything?"

He gave an offhand shrug as if he didn't care. "I was able to save the old homestead by declaring bankruptcy, but just barely. I had to auction off most of my stock, double-mortgage the old home place . . . "

What about your parents? Do you have any family?"

"My folks are both dead." His blue eyes were clouded with sadness as they met hers.

"Jake, I'm sorry."

"I wouldn't have wanted them to watch everything go. I've got four younger brothers, but they moved on after college. I'm the last one in the family dairy business.""Oh, Jake," she said gently. She understood hard work and disappointment all too well. She'd grown up in a respectable but poor family—six children supported by the meager income of a tailor and a waitress. "So," she said briskly. "You become a slum lord here."

"A what?" he asked blankly. He blinked hard. "Oh, no. I'm fixin' the place up. I wouldn't rent it to people the way it is now. See, my Uncle Needham left me this buildin' in his will. I'm goin' to get it in shape, rent the apartments out, and then try to sell the whole shebang."

"Is there a Mrs. Jake?" Vivian asked. "And little Jakettes?"

"Nope." He cut his eyes and mimicked her. "Is there a Mr. Judge—poor, henpecked soul—or anything smaller than you that calls you 'Mama?'"

"No."

"Never married?"

"I've been divorced for three years. Now, Redneck, you don't need to ask all these personal questions . . . "

"Don't go changin' the subject, Tough stuff. Why'd you kick the poor man out?"

"I didn't. He ran."

"Hmmm." Jake tucked his chin and looked at her for a silent moment. "Did you love him?"

"Mr. Coltrane, I don't think this falls under the questions the doctor had in mind."

"You want me to make trouble?" he quipped. His eyes gleamed as his voice dropped to a stage whisper. "Oh, doctor, come quick! The poor lady over here's talkin' to her toes and askin' where to catch the next MARTA to the Starship Enterprise."

"All right, all right." She yielded, feeling exasperated. This situation made for an unusual intimacy between strangers, and he appeared determined to get answers from her. Vivian tilted her chin up as best she could and looked him directly in the eye. "Yes, at the time I loved him. Yes, it was hard not to be hurt when you come home from work one night and find your husband's gone off to join the circus."

He did a quick double take.

"He fell in love with a trapeze performer from Cirque de Soleil. I was working long hours as a public defender for the city. We just lost touch."

"Any boyfriends?"

"I don't have any, but I can't vouch for *him*."

Jake chuckled. "Well, why *don't* you have any boyfriends?"

"A woman without a man is like a tuna without a bicycle."

"Maybe you just been fishing in all the wrong creeks."

"Wow, dog, you know how to flirt," she said in a syrupy voice.

"I try to do my duty to the female of the species. But enough about me. How old are you?"

"Young enough to be interested and old enough to know better. I'm not on the market anymore. "

"Nah, you've got potential. Maybe it's something only a man could see." His deep baritone took on a very patient tone. "Now, darlin', tell me how many years old . . . "

"I'm thirty-two. And don't say I'm too young to be a city court judge."

"I was about to say you're prime meat on the hoof."

Her eyes narrowed. "I usually get a kiss after such flowery flattery."

Jake leaned over closely, holding her hypnotized. "Okay." He gave her a gentle kiss. His lips were warm and firm, and he pursed them just right, just enough to tug at her own when he pulled away. Her involuntary but obviously appreciative sigh followed him.

"I'm thirty-four," he told her. "So this thing ought to work out real well." He settled back on his stool.

She was speechless. A few seconds later, it occurred to her that she must look like a scared squirrel, staring numbly at him over the fluffy wool collar of his coat.

"*What* ought to work out real well?" she managed,

her voice sounding unreal to her.

"Us going out on a date."

"I'm not a fish. You didn't bait a hook and catch me."

"A little small, but a keeper."

"I said I'm not on the market."

"I'm just askin' you to dinner, not running you through the check-out scanner."

"What are you yelling about?" Maria asked in exasperation a moment later, appearing by Vivian's side.

"Is Washington still around?"

"Yes . . . "

"Ask him if he can give me a ride home."

Maria flipped a cell phone open and made a call.

"I'll take you home," Jake interjected calmly.

"I don't think that would be a good idea." Vivian sat up and handed Jake his coat. She felt Maria's sharp eyes assessing her and the situation. Vivian brushed her fingers through her tangled hair, trying to calm down.

"This yokel upsetting you, Viv?"

"He's no problem. A good guy. Just a little freakin' possessive."

"I'll call security."

"No."

"Vivian," Jake said quietly, "I brought you here, and I can be trusted to drive you home."

"No, thanks. But if you ever need a traffic ticket fixed, I'll see what I can do. Good night."

Abruptly, Barney Washington arrived in the small space. "Somebody said you need a ride home, Your Honor," he offered, eyeing the scene curiously.

"Yes, I do." She wobbled off the gurney and headed for a corridor, trailed closely by the officer and

Jake. Vivian felt strangely close to crying again. She wanted to whirl around and thump Jake Coltrane on his broad chest and ask why he wanted to complicate her life with laughter and kindness and passion.

She had formed a tough skin for all the pitiful, ugly, disgusting things in her work and in her life, and now he wanted to tear it all to hell. It was bad enough that when Barney Washington and Maria spread word of this goofy incident to the Municipal Court offices, she'd never live this night down.

Jake stopped by the double doors to the ambulance ramp and watched Vivian careen out as Washington held the door for her.

He'd ruffled her feathers, and he was sorry for not understanding the depth of her cynicism toward men. His hopes sank all the way to his heels, and he cursed himself for not taking things slower.

"What's the rush?" a bleary-eyed wino called from a nearby corner. "Somebody lose somethin' important?" Officer Washington still held the door open. Vivian stopped just outside, her breath frosty in the winter air, and twisted around to stare at Jake with an expression that was both sad and determined. "I really do thank you for what you did. I really do appreciate it. But I'm kind of a loner. Good night."

His heart pulled into a pained knot.

Vivian had forgotten to take off his cap, and brown-black hair tumbled thickly to her shoulders beneath it. She raised one hand in a tiny wave.

"I'll never forget what you did," she called raggedly.

The door swung shut between them.

Chapter Three

"Let me get this straight, sir." Vivian idly touched the two-day-old lump on her head, stretched her black robed arms out in front of her and clasped her hands together. A short man with a pinched face looked up at her. A bored police officer and an attorney from the prosecutor's office slouched behind him. "You say a photograph of Kanye West spoke to you from the window at Barnes and Noble?"

"Told me to let my light shine!"

"Are you sure you don't want legal counsel?"

"Hah! I spit at convention!"

"Very commendable. However, the ladies who reported you to the police said you spat at *them*, and then your light has remarkable resemblance to your middle finger. Could that be true?"

"Anything could be true, Judge. The poles are about the shift." He swirled his hands. "Whole planet gonna turn upside down in a few years. Nostradamus said so. So did the Mayans, way back when."

She cocked one brow at the arresting officer, a young blond with a handlebar mustache. "Why wasn't this man sent to the psychiatric ward at Grady?"

"We took him over there. They said if they admitted everybody who says weird stuff they'd have to commit half the city and most of Mayor Franklin's staff."

"Here's the report," the court secretary whispered

from the desk to Vivian's left. Vivian looked down at Callender Remington's pretty face and saw discomfort. "I forgot," Callendar added anxiously. "I mean, 'Here's the report, Your Honor.'"

"No problem."

The tall redhead smiled sadly, thanking her. Cal was a prime example of how to let a man mess up your life, Vivian told herself silently. She was fighting to keep her husband, a lovable but irresponsible young golf player on the pro circuit, from spending the two of them into bankruptcy. The strain was showing.

Thinking of Cal's financial problems made Vivian think of farmers in debt, and farmers in debt made her think of Jake Coltrane. But then, everything during the two days since their encounter made her think of Jake Coltrane. *Thank God it's Friday and I can spend the weekend getting back to normal,* Vivian noted, touching her sore head. She glanced at the medical report in her hand, frowning.

"Okay, Nostradamus," she snapped. The man tittered. "Plead guilty to one count of misdemeanor assault and I'll send you to Grady for observation. You'll get a couple of hot meals and a cozy bed for the night."

He grinned. "Works every time."

Vivian thumped her gavel.

"I'll tell Nostradamus you said hello," he assured her as the police officer led him away.

The defendant in the next case was late, so they shuffled papers for a minute. A pair of attorneys lounged by Vivian's huge desk on its carpeted dais. Detectives and police officers ambled in and out. A room full of more than twenty rough-looking people waited to be arraigned over the course of the afternoon session. Tom Crawford, the court clerk, moved restlessly at the desk to her right. Angular, tall, sporting a short version of a Don King afro, Tom leaned toward her. He had a wicked sense of humor.

"Did that good ol' boy who helped you out the other night chew tobacco and dip snuff?" he asked in a low voice, grinning.

Shaking her head at the way the stores about Jake Coltrane were growing, Vivian sighed.

"He was very nice and very polite. We could use more of that around here, you know."

"I'd give twenty bucks to have seen his face when he unwrapped you. It's probably been years since he saw a woman wearing anything but overalls."

"He didn't ogle me, if that's what you're hinting at. He was an old-fashioned gentleman," Vivian said firmly.

"Heard he tried to hit on you. And you hit back."

Vivian's stomach jumped. A detective who'd been listening plopped one arm on Tom's desk and spoke in a conspiratorial whisper.

"I heard the guy's a cross between Larry the Cable Guy and Huck Finn." They shared low, masculine snickers. Vivian blanched.

"That's enough," she ordered. "All right, where's my pimping case?"

An undercover detective ambled through the double doors at the back of the small room, chewing gum. He wore army fatigues, a ski sweater, and sunglasses.

"Your honor, are you waitin' on Schwartz, Malcom E.?" he asked.

"Yeah."

"Hospitalized." He put a finger to his chest and

pulled an imaginary trigger. "Ka-boom. One of his ladies plugged him this morning."

"One down," Vivian muttered under her breath. "Thank you, detective." Without missing a beat, she handed the Schwartz invoices to Cal. Shootings were so commonplace that Vivian didn't take time to register surprise or even curiosity.

"My pleasure," the detective purred, looking at Cal. Vivian glanced up in time to see him leer at her. *Men. Hormone-driven dogs.*

"Take your spastic eyebrows out of my court, Detective."

He smiled. "Yes, Your Honor. Good work the other night, Your Honor. Heard you got your man."

Before she could threaten to charge him with contempt, he disappeared into the dirty, concrete-walled corridor outside. Vivian turned over a cupful of pens with a disconcerted movement of her hand.

Jake Coltrane might as well have branded her with a hot cattle iron. Everyone seemed to think she belonged to him.

03 • 80

Jake stopped on the courthouse's stairs, keeping a tight grip on the big, muscle-bound young man who gasped beside him. An arrow on a red-lettered sign pointed to a scuffed, steel door on the next landing. The sign cautioned: PUBLIC DEFENDER. NO WEAPONS.

"Just leave me here and get somebody to carry me, man. I can't make it up any more steps," his captive whined. "We're never gonna find municipal court like this."

"I'll turn you loose when chickens lay square eggs." Jake dragged the burly character back down the slick steps. The guy hobbled quickly, his hands and feet bound with rows of baling wire. Jake kept one rock-hard arm around his neck.

They maneuvered up the last set of stairs, through the security door, then down a narrow, stained hallway into another part of the building, where Jake found a lobby.

Jake was thankful no officers stopped him to ask questions. *In the afternoon crowd wandering around this place we're about the most normal pair*, he thought in amazement, as a surly, heavily tattooed man bumped him and uttered an obscenity.

How could Viv—that was the intimate way he thought of her now, *Viv*—work in this joint? No wonder she had to act so tough and snappy.

Directions to the five municipal court chambers upstairs were posted over two creaking elevators. Jake exhaled in relief and guided his prisoner toward them. They trundled through yet another set of security scanners.

"See, man, I told you we should have come in this way instead of creeping in the back door," the man sniped during the elevator ride. "Dumb redneck."

"Not so dumb that I couldn't catch *you*," Jake reminded him as they left the elevator, went through more security checkpoints, then worked their way to an information desk.

"Where's Judge Costa's courtroom, ma'am?" he asked an officer.

She stared at him and his baling-wire-wrapped prisoner. "What the . . . how did you . . . who are . . . didn't anyone ask you for I.D. downstairs? What department are you from?"

Uh oh. "I'm makin' a citizen's arrest."

She nearly shrieked. "You just walked in *off the street?*"

"That's what citizens do, ma'am."

"Not in *this* city, mister."

She was reaching for the call button on her shoulder radio when Officer Washington walked up. "I know this farmer. It's cool, Shaneeqa."

Jake looked at him gratefully while giving his prisoner a little shake. "I brought Viv a present. Figured this is more subtle than roses and a bottle of champagne."

Barney Washington's dark, surprised eyes filled with sly amusement. "Awright, man. I'll ride this train to Trouble Town with you. Come on."

He led Jake and the hobbling criminal through a set of double doors identified by a COURTROOM 3 sign.

Jake gazed happy at Vivian Costas, looking small but official behind the courtroom's raised desk. She was studying the screen of a computer and didn't see him come in. Her black hair was tucked up in a knot on the back of her head. The front of it fluffed away from her face in layers. Even in a voluminous black robe with a prim white collar peaking out the top, she looked enticing. Jake took a deep breath then lugged his captive up the center aisle.

The scraggly crowd lounging in the courtroom benches turned to stare. Someone sputtered. "That's police brutality if I ever seen it!"

"He can be brutal to me *any* time," crooned a woman in tight purple hot pants and a tank top. "Oooh, baby, your place, my place, any place. Tickle my fancy, you big ol' hunk of flannel-covered sausage."

Jake's face was grim as he shoved his charge ahead of him. A detective yawned and turned from Vivian's desk to slowly scan him.

"You work vice, don't you, man?" he asked Jake. "I think you're supposed to take this guy next door."

"This Duddly Do-Right doesn't work vice!" Jake's captive burst out in exasperation. "Get him off me, man! He's just some crazy mofo out there doin' a Rambo on people."

"Your Honor," Jake said firmly. "Viv. . . "

Her head came up quickly at the sound of his voice. He noted happily that for just a fleeting second her eyes lit with what might have been delight, and their glow sent shivers through his body. Then her mouth popped open and her face turned bright scarlet.

"I brought you a present, Your Honor," Jake said solemnly. He nodded toward his prisoner. "This is one of 'em, isn't it? I got a good look at him the other night, but you need to identify . . . "

"Mr. Coltrane," she said tightly, her voice wavering. He blinked in surprise at the rebuking tone. "Mr. Coltrane," she repeated more definitely, "you cannot just barge in here with a man trussed up like a bale of hay. We have procedures for this sort of thing, and you have just circumvented all of them. You should have turned this man over to a police officer." She peered around him, glaring at Barney Washington, who stood at the back of the room, trying to look innocent.

"I made a citizen's arrest," Jake protested. In Tuna Creek, no one questions a citizen's duty to help the law out from time to time. You can split hairs all you want . . . Your Honor . . . but the fact is that this joker is one of the creeps who attacked you."

She blinked rapidly, frowning harder as her gaze went to the man Jake held. Her eyes narrowed to grim slits as she recognized him. Her breath made a slow hiss. Her hands, resting on the computer's keyboard, trembled then clenched.

"Mr. Coltrane," she said formally, straightening her shoulders, "the court appreciates your help, and the arrest is duly noted." She motioned for one of the uniformed officers to come over. The officer rushed forward. "I'm going to file aggravated assault charges against this man," she told the officer. "The baled-up one, not the other, despite the fact that he's disrupted the court with his irresponsible actions . . . "

"Aw, don't be mean, your honor," the purple-panted hooker called from the pews. "If a man did something that nice for me, I'd take him home and—"

"Order!" Vivian thumped her gavel down.

Tom Crawford had one arm flung casually across her desk, holding out a document. She hit his fingertips by accident. Tom yelped. Vivian's face went white as the spectators and most of the detectives repressed giggles.

"Viv," Jake began desperately. "Your Honor, I mean. I thought I was doin' the right thing." He spread his big hands in front of him, the gesture beseeching and frustrated. "I don't know the rules here. I just know that men who beat up women shouldn't be out on the streets. That's no different here than anywhere else. But I apologize for upsettin' you . . . upsettin' the court, I mean. I sure didn't start out to do that."

He stuck his hands into the pockets of his rugged coat and gazed at her in silence for a moment. She looked back, shaking her head slowly, her expression formal and reserved. She seemed about to pop with anger.

"The court thanks you again," she said finally. Her voice had no tone at all. He nodded dully.

Well, that was that.

He tipped a finger to his forehead in good-bye and turned on his heel, striding down the aisle. An old man leaned out of a pew and hissed at him wordlessly, toothlessly. Several women in the audience made little kissing sounds and laughed.

Jake squared his back and felt miserable.

Vivian watched him go with tear-filled eyes.

I've never met anyone like you before,, Jake Coltrane. What am I going to do?

ଓ • ଓ

Like its owner, Jake Coltrane's little apartment building was sturdy, basic and old-fashioned.

Vivian slowly climbed the wide concrete steps. Her eyes assessed the fading red brick and confused architectural styles—the arched, Spanish-style windows, most of them boarded over, the ornate cornice, the gated alcove that led into a courtyard at the main entrance. She estimated the two-story building was split into about six apartments, upstairs and down.

She glanced up and down the street. Small bungalows and old Victorians crowded up to the narrow, tree-lined sidewalks. Some of the homes were freshly renovated, others were still shabby. The whole street looked that way—a mixture of hope and despair, the future and the past. Vivian tested the complex's peeling, wrought-iron gate, fingering the new padlock and chain.

Peering through the bars, she saw an old fountain surrounded by patchy winter grass and a few scraggly shrubs. But the shrubs had been carefully pruned and were necklaced in rich mounds of fresh soil and mulch.

Jake's work. It must be. What would a farmer do first after inheriting a run-down building in the middle of the city?

Tend to his land, of course.

Vivian looked up at the apartment on the front side of the building to her right. Its windows weren't boarded over, and light shown through them.

"What now? Should I throw a rock at his window panes?" she asked aloud in the fading winter light. "Is that how women come calling in Tuna Creek? He'll probably shoot first and ask questions later."

The sound of scurrying paws startled her. In the dusk, two huge dogs raced across the courtyard toward the gate. They barked—no, they *bellowed*—their canine voices deep and rolling. Vivian backed away s they reared and placed thick paws against the gate. She remembered them vaguely from the other night.

A door slammed overhead, and she heard feet hurrying down metal stairs. The monstrous hounds leaped away to greet the sound. A few seconds later, they reappeared, their tales wagging. Jake was between them. Vivian gasped and put one hand up as the bright beam of his flashlight blinded her.

"I'll talk, I'll talk," she quipped tartly. "Only call off the dogs!"

Wordlessly, Jake clicked the light off. Setting a shotgun to one side, he unlocked the gate and held it open.

She eased through, pushing gingerly at the snuffling noses that pressed into her quilted blue coat. Her heart beating a rapid tattoo, Vivian looked up at him. What little she could see of his expression in the dusk looked wary, defensive. He had on jeans and a ribbed, scoop-necked white sweater. *No*, she corrected. *It isn't a sweater. It's the top to long underwear.*

In any case, he had a magnificent, muscular chest.

She watched it swell as he took a deep breath.

"Can I help you with somethin', Your Honor?" he asked. "Are you makin' a citizen's arrest? Awright, I admit it. I left a Dunkin' Donuts coffee cup in the back of my truck, and I'm pretty sure it blew out when I wasn't looking. You're too wily for the likes of my criminal mind. I confess. You got me." He held out his wrists. "For litterin'."

"Would you please accept my sincere 'Thank you,' for what you did today?"

His lips parted in surprise. He searched her face with such intensity that she looked away and pretended to study the courtyard's ornamental tiles. They were neatly washed and showed signs of new mortar.

"You know, I don't mind that people made fun of me in your courtroom," he said. "But I *did* mind that no one, not even you, said it's a good thing for people to look out for each other. That's what justice is really about, at least to me. The fair and honest keeping of the peace. All that 'Do unto others' talk in the Bible."

"Jake." She touched his arm and looked up at him with remorse. "You have to understand. As a judge, I can't encourage citizens to take the law into their own hands. But as a human being, personally? I thought what you did was . . . it was noble."

"You did?" His smile grew then became mischievous. "Noble, huh?"

"But I had to do what courtroom protocol dictated. I had to be cool."

He grinned down at her as if he could barely contain himself. *The man is so open-hearted and vulnerable*, Vivian thought wistfully. "But I don't have to be cool now. And so I hope you'll let me buy you dinner tonight. How about it?"

Vivian's fingers still rested lightly on his forearm. Abruptly skittish, she dropped her and took a step back.

His grin widened even more. They stared at each other, two lonely people together in the retreating daylight. "I accept," he said.

"This is crazy," she whispered huskily. "We have nothing in common. You probably drink buttermilk."

"Can't stand the stuff," he whispered back. "I like my milk like I like my women.

"Cold and fresh?"

"Sweet and smooth."

"I'm not sweet, Jake. I'm sarcastic and cynical," she warned softly. "I don't want any man to complicate my life. It took me a long time to get my act together after my husband left."

"We're just going to dinner," he reminded her. "You're not expecting anything else, are you? 'Cause I'm not that kind of boy."

"Oh, really."

"I never complicate women's lives over just a single first dinner."

"You're too trusting."

"No, I give people a chance. Innocent till proven guilty, right?"

"Right," she murmured slowly. Her eyes flickered to his lips, then up to meet his languid gaze and back down.

"I think we'd better walk to dinner," she said, and chuckled weakly. "I need the air."

"When you smile like that, you have the prettiest dimple, Your Honor."

"Back off," she growled. "It's not a dimple, it's a smirk."

He laughed. "Wait right here while I get my coat." He tilted his head with just the right mix of teasing and invitation. "Unless you want to come up and see my collection of *Dairy Farms Today* magazines? And I have a complete set of 'Legends of NASCAR' commemorative plates. You don't see a gold-rimmed Dale Earnhardt platter too often."

Vivian gazed up at him in mesmerized silence. "I'm more of a modern dance and soccer type. You have any gold-rimmed 'Legends of Soccer' plates?"

He put his hands on his hips. "No, but I have a muddy Atlanta *Falcons* pendant signed by Terance Mathis."

"Who?"

He looked heavenward. "Mama, I'm sorry, but she's a heathen."

Shaking his head and laughing, he trotted back upstairs. His hounds loped after him. He came back down in less than a minute, his red-gold hair hastily brushed, a flannel shirt half-buttoned over his ribbed top, slipping his coat on hurriedly as he cleared the steps.

They smiled awkwardly at each other. Once they reached the sidewalk he swiftly placed himself between her and the street then grasped Vivian's elbow. Vivian jumped.

He let go. But his mouth quirked. "I'm not doing anything I wouldn't do the same if I was walkin' my own grandma, may she rest in peace."

"I can hold my own elbow, but thanks."

He chortled.

They strolled to funky tapas bar a couple of blocks over, in a section of midtown that had been revitalized by art galleries and restaurants. By the time their dinner arrived, Vivian had learned that Jake had a bachelor's degree in agribusiness from the University of Tennessee, that he had read all the Harry Potter novels, that he could clog, line dance and play a fiddle, and that his cousin from Nashville had caused him to fall out of a hayloft once and break his nose, which was why it crooked slightly to the right now.

"Kids get into trouble like that growing up in the city, too," Vivian told him over imported beer and olives wrapped in serrano ham. "When I was five, Valerie Jacobi tried to rearrange my kneecaps with a baseball bat. She was six and mean as hell. But she's doing time for mail fraud now, so I can afford to forgive and forget."

He laughed, amazed.

"How old were you when your cousin dumped you out of the hayloft?" Vivian asked, smiling crookedly. His rich laughter was like the music of a bass saxophone—mellow and deadly seductive.

"Thirty-three," he replied, still laughing.

"Then it was last year! You overdeveloped adolescent."

"It was my cousin's fault," Jake insisted. "He's older than I am. He talked me into going up there with him and drinking whiskey under a full moon."

"You were celebrating something?"

His laughter faded, and although a smile still played around his mouth, pain edged its way into his blue eyes.

"No. Rylan had just broken up with a woman, and the last extension had just run out on my bank loan. We had things to forget."

He pretended to study his beer glass while she studied him.

"I picture you with your shotgun," Vivian said

softly. "Standing in your driveway and daring anybody to tell you to shut down your dairy."

"No." He shook his head, smiling pensively now, his eyes still riveted to the glass. "When I look back on it, I wish I had done that. But I didn't and I'm not goin' to sit around regrettin' the past now. I had to sell off a lot of equipment and some of the stock, but at least I was able to keep the farm."

His words were stoic but she sensed defeat and depression behind them. "You hate it here, don't you?" she asked gently. "In the city."

He looked up at her then, tilting his head to one side, his expression thoughtful.

"Yeah. I can't breathe. The closeness of it, the concrete, the noise. Whew. But the people aren't so bad, just a little suspicious—and always in such a hurry . . . " His hand rested on top of hers. "In fact, certain people might be worth it."

The implication caused in her an overload of responses both physical and emotional. They were too intense, and she retreated. Her hand stiffened under his, and she withdrew it.

"Jake, you don't have to flatter me."

"It's not flattery." Vivian met his eyes and found them serious. He nodded. "I don't make up pretty words to get women to like me. If I tell you something, I mean it. I don't mean to rattle you all the time."

"You do not 'rattle' me," she answered proudly. "You . . . you invade my space. I need my space."

They stared at each other a moment. When the corner of Jake's mouth twitched with amusement, she couldn't help rolling her eyes.

"This ain't an invasion, darlin'," he drawled. "It's a romance."

"It's just a dinner."

"It's a date. You asked me out on a *date*, girl."

"Did not."

"Did to."

"Okay, the jury's still out. Let's leave it at that."

"You have to act reserved, I know," he replied. "Anybody who does what you do for a livin' has to keep her dignity. But you don't have to be scared of me lying to you, embarrassing you or otherwise deliberately hurtin' you."

"I'm not afraid of men hurting me," she lied. He had a way of zooming right to the truth. "And certainly not you. You wouldn't hurt a fly."

"Well, now, hold on. I don't want you to think I'm harmless. Why, I've broken hearts all over Tennessee. There are women who'll never be the same because of me."

"My hair stylist says the same thing."

"Why you sassy little heifer . . . "

"Call the police, would you?" a well-dressed man ordered as he walked past their table. He directed his waspish instruction at a waitress with a wave of one tanned hand. "There's an old boozer huddled by my car, and he won't leave."

"That's Roberto," the waitress replied nervously. "You just need to ask him politely . . . "

"If he scratches the paint job on my Lexus I'll *politely* run over him. Can't you have the police come pick him up?"

Vivian leaped to her feet. Jake stood too, angling in front of her. She looked around him at the waitress. "I thought Roberto went to live with his sister in Miami."

She ran for the door, and Jake hurried after her.

Chapter Four

Roberto had a heedful of wild white hair, a growling Spanish accent, and a scowl that could scare pit bulls. He was medium-sized, or looked medium-sized, at least—he was sitting cross-legged on the curb, so Jake had trouble telling. His clothes were old but in fairly good condition. A battered army duffle sagged beside him. When he smiled up at Vivian, Jake saw in surprise that he had a decent set of teeth. Vivian clucked like a mother hen, knelt beside Roberto, and slipped an arm around his shoulders.

"Mr. Marino, I thought you blew this joint in October," she told him, shaking her head. "What happened to the Miami thing?"

"My sister, she married this guy who thought that I should go on the welfare. Forget that!" He thumped his knee for emphasis. "A Vietnam veteran on welfare!"

"I'm sorry," she said sympathetically.

"So, anyhow. We had this big blow-up and I got on the bus to Atlanta last week. Figured I could get my old job back at the Farmer's Market. But they're laying people off. Don't need me." He held out his other hand, showing her a bruised forefinger. "Then, last night, some *pendejo* rolled me down at the mission. Look at this. Finger's busted. I'm busted." He angled his thumb at Jake. "Who's he?"

"He's a friend of mine. Roberto Marino, meet Jake Coltrane."

Jake squatted on his heels and held out a hand. Roberto squinted at it, grunted, and extended his good hand, which was as work-hardened as Jakes. They shook solemnly.

"You look like some sort of crawdad back in here between these cars," Jake said, smiling.

Roberto shot him a bewildered and somewhat offended look, then turned to Vivian for help. He asked out of the side of his mouth. "Is that good, Vivvy?"

"It's okay," Vivian assured him. She shook her head, looked at Jake with a wry smile, then back at Roberto. She felt like an interpreter at the UN.

"If you say so," Roberto acknowledged. "So, how've you been, Vivvy? Who you been helpin' out lately, you pretty babe, you?"

"*You*, it looks like," she answered. "Did you take a leak on this car?" She pointed to the Lexus next to him and glanced at the tire in a totally businesslike manner.

"Would Roberto Marino stoop to that?" Roberto's voice rose. "No! I only told the *pendejo* I *would* water his tires if he didn't watch his mouth."

"Okay. I knew that guy was just a jerk."

Jake ran a hand through his hair and then dropped his chin to hide his amusement. He remembered what Officer Washington had called her that night at Grady: A patron saint who cared about people.

"Well." Vivian squeezed Roberto's shoulders again. She gazed up at the starlit night, pensive. "Let's see what we can come up with . . . " Her eyes rolled slowly over to Jake. A satisfied smile curved her full lips into calculated charm. "Mr. Coltrane, you have such a wonderful, needy place, and Roberto knows all about carpentry work . . . "

She let her voice trail off. Her eyes stayed on him, pleading, hoping, focusing all her energy into rendering him helpless.

"You had me at 'needy,'" Jake mumbled, running his hand through his hair again and sighing.

"Thank you!"

Jake stood and held out both hands, one to help Vivian, one to help his new tenant.

"Roberto," he said drily, "you're my official first tenant."

ભ • ଖ

Back at Jake's apartments, Roberto drank three glasses of milk, ate a huge bowl of vegetable soup, and downed two tuna-salad sandwiches. Then he went into Jake's living room with a pillow and an armful of hand-made quilts that had been in the Coltrane family for half a century, and promptly went to sleep on the couch, snoring softly.

Jake shut the double doors to the living room, crossed a narrow hallway, entered the kitchen, and sat down by Vivian at a massive oak dining table. Vivian smiled at him between sips of coffee.

"This is a terrific place. You've done an excellent job on it."

"Thank you. I'm clean, but not much for decoratin'."

She eyed all the careful work that had restored the high ceilings and cabinets. Colorful, braided rugs adorned the wood floors. The kitchen appliances were old but functional. Family portraits in gilded frames decorated the pale beige walls.

"Where are the bedrooms?"

She had meant it without innuendo, but realized too late that it was a strange question to blurt out. "I mean, how many are there?"

"Three," he said just as awkwardly. "Two little ones, one big one. I have the big one." They looked at each other with wide eyes. Pink stained the ruddy tan on his cheeks. Vivian burst into laughter.

"I'm go glad for you," she sputtered.

He laughed then, too, rubbed his jaw as if to coax the blush away, and then propped his chin on his hand. "You swear that Roberto knows carpentry?"

"Yes, I swear." Vivian grinned at him. "He used to work part-time at one of the city shelters. That's where he and I met. He'll work hard if you treat him with respect."

"You know, Viv, I thought all homeless people were . . . I don't know. . . "
"Panhandling bums or addicts or mentally ill bag lades," she finished, nodding. "But they're not. A lot of them are people like Roberto—good people, down on their luck, who just don't fit in easily but will work hard if given the chance."

"And you want me to believe you're hard-hearted." He made a chiding sound in his throat. "You're just a little ol' Moon Pie."

"I'm not old," she retorted playfully.

"No, ma'am, you're prime."
"A Moon Pie, huh? Damn. Hard on the outside, soft on the inside?"

"Are you talkin' dirty to me?"
She suddenly focused her attention on her coffee mug, aware that every part of her anatomy even vaguely related to male-female functions had just gone on alert; her nipples felt hard against the lace of her bra. She held up the heavy pottery mug, studying it and trying to think of a way to change the subject. She felt Jake's

eyes on her.

"I love anything that's made by hand," she ventured.

He guffawed.

"Look!" she exclaimed, squaring her shoulders and affecting a placid face as she continued to hold the mug aloft, "My Statue of Liberty impression."

They both laughed, the tension broken.

"Tough Stuff, I can't remember when I've had such a good time," he told her. He took the empty mug from her and set it down. His blue eyes captured the soft light of an old lamp perched on the kitchen counter nearby. Vivian thought of a vivid blue ocean, an ocean that drew her hypnotically, an ocean where drowning would be a sweet adventure. Jake raised one broad hand and touched her cheek gently.

"You make me laugh at myself," he murmured. His fingers stroked her cheekbone with a feather-light touch, then moved down her jaw. She looked at him transfixed, and her hands trembled as she put them in her lap. "You make me fight back, Viv. You make me feel mad and confused and crazy and happy. You make me feel better than I have in a long, long time."

"I can cook," she replied blankly. Vivian barely knew what she was saying. His forefinger grazed her mouth and she kissed it, then his thumb, then his palm, her lips damp and agile as she sampled his callused skin. Their eyes remained locked. He placed his finger tips against her neck, stroking her pulse. His thumb rested lightly on the corner of her mouth, drawing tiny circles.

"Why, that's real nice to know," he quipped softly, seductively.

"I make great cannelloni," she continued with

languid tones. "I . . . I have a collection of Tony Bennett albums. I work out with weights three times a week at the YMCA. I love the *Ice Age* movies. I sleep late on the weekends . . . "

Her next words were lost, caught in a moan as he leaned forward, his chair creaking, and kissed her deeply. She tilted her head at one angle and then another, making exciting little discoveries about his taste and feel as their tongues curled in and out, playing a sensual game of tag.

Vivian drew back and smiled at him warily, catching her breath. "I'm not much for casual hook ups."

"Me, neither."

"Jake . . . " Another kiss stopped her. When he finally let her draw a shaky breath, she continued. "You're trouble."

"Yep." He pulled her out of her chair and onto his lap. With a gruff sound, he pressed his mouth against her neck. Vivian nearly burst with pleasure as he fervently kissed the tender skin under her jaw.

She nuzzled the side of his head and hugged him. They were both trembling.

He began to chuckle, and rested his forehead against her shoulder. He patted her back with one broad hand.

She gripped his shoulder, and when he looked up she gave him a serious once-over that went beyond joking. Vivian urged quietly, "Tell the truth. How many women are regular visitors here at your corn crib?"

Jake gave her a wicked grin. "If I told you I love the jealous glint in your eyes, would you hit me?"

"Right in the teeth."

He planted a loud, smacking kiss on the straight

line of her lips.

"The last time I even came close to have female company of the sort you mean was back in the fall," he related solemnly. "An old girlfriend drove down from Tennessee to help me move in here. She took one look at this place and got back in her pick-up truck and left."

It was Vivian's turn to laugh. She saw defensive pride flow into his handsome face, flattening his brows into a frown. She shook her head before it became more intense.

"Jake, I'm laughing because I'm in shock, that's all."

"Oh." A sheepish smile replaced his grim expression. He waved a nonchalant hand, and his voice became comically nostalgic. "She was a right bossy heifer, but good-hearted. I've known her since we were in grade school. Once when we were about, oh, eight years old, she caught me at the playground and pulled my pants down. I learned to do an Olympic sprint with my dungarees around my ankles that day."

"Stop, stop," Vivian commanded, thumping his shoulders and laughing. She settled her arms cozily around his neck, and he bounced her once on his knee. His laughter joined hers. "Was that typical of your romances in Tuna Creek? Come on, confess."

His rumbling laughter faded like distant spring thunder. Now his eyes were pensive.

"I never dated a woman I couldn't live without." He shrugged. "One told me I was gettin' set in my ways and wouldn't ever find anybody." His voice dropped "I guess I got pretty borin' in the years after my wife left. I sort of withdrew."

"Wife?" Her smile faded.

"I got married right out of college. Three years later

she packed up and left for Nashville. She wanted to be a singer."

"Did she make it?"

"Yeah, she did pretty well. She sings backup for some big names, does commercials, that sort of thing. She remarried, had kids. I'm proud of her."

Vivian frowned. "Do you find good things to say about everybody?"

"Try it. It keeps your blood pressure down. When somebody hurts you real bad, find a way to forgive. It cleans your soul. We were just kids when we got married. Looking back on it, I think what we had together just bottomed out."

They head the mournful howl of a dog coming from a back bedroom. Vivian climbed off his lap before he could hold her still. She was still processing the wife story.

Jake sighed and stood up. "Phoebe probably pushed Chester off the bed."

She busied herself grabbing her coat. "I'll leave you to your threesome. Well, your foursome, if you count Roberto."

"I don't sleep with my dogs. They got their own bed. They hog the covers."

He took her hand. Vivian avoided the inquiring blue gaze he beamed down on her. "Will you go out with me this weekend, Viv? I'll buy pizza and take you to a movie."

"I'm flying down to Florida in the morning to spend the weekend with my brother, Frank, and his family."

He looked crest-fallen. "What about one night next week, Viv?"

"I'm a member of the mayor's committee on

midtown crime. I have meetings every night through Thursday."

"Well, at least I know you're not faking me out. That's the most boring excuse I've ever heard."

"Why don't you give me a call next week sometime," she allowed, "and we'll see."

"Viv, tell me the truth." He looked straight into her eyes. "Are you givin' me the heave-ho?"

"I'm giving you my schedule. If I were giving you the heave-ho, I'd be a lot more direct, dude."

"Okay, then." He lifted her like a delicate china doll and planted a happy kiss on her startled mouth, then set her down. Vivian wobbled with shaky knees to the door that led to the stair landing above the courtyard, and he slid her blue coat onto her arms.

"I'll walk you to your car."

"You don't have to do that, Jake."

"Yes, I do. What kind of men are you used to, who let you go traipsin' around city streets by yourself after a date?"

"I can take care of myself."

"By whacking thugs with a shoulder bag full of law books?" he teased, following her as she went down the outside stairs to the courtyard.

"My street name is Sistah B Bad."

They shared a laugh.

"You know, that fellow I caught said his partner skipped town." Jake's voice turned deadly serious.

"Good. I don't want you playing policeman any more. Those guys are sociopaths. You could get killed."

"Huh. If that second guy ever shows his face around her again, I'll be the ruthless one."

Vivian stopped, threw her arms around Jake's neck, and hugged him so tightly that he coughed. She pulled away quickly, ducked her head to hide the tears in her eyes, and walked on.

This time she didn't pull away when he tucked his big hand firmly under her elbow as they went down the concrete steps to the sidewalk. They stopped in front of her tiny silver hybrid. He chortled. "This must fit real good on your kitchen counter. I bet you plug it in right next to the charger for your cell phone."

She snorted as she retrieved the keys from her purse, and Jake immediately took them from her hand. She looked up at him in mild rebuke. He didn't say a word as he unlocked and then opened her door. He politely returned her keys.

She arched a brow. "You think all this mannerly crap will make me kiss you again?"

He put his hands on his lean hips. "Yeah."

"You're right." She slid her arms around his neck. He drew her into his arms, bent his head over hers, and bestowed a long, intimate kiss on her parted lips. She kissed him back hungrily, and her body edged closer to his.

They held each other for a long moment, in which Vivian analyzed her tangled emotions and found equal measures of love at first sight and fear that he was too good to be true. "G'night," she said breathlessly, and pushed him away.

As she slid behind the wheel of her car, her eyes never left Jake's face.

"Y'all come back now, you hear?" he said with a grand drawl, grinning crookedly.

She gave him a pensive half-smile that made no promises.

Ϡ • ϡ

Vivian's office was small and cramped, overflowing

with law books and memorabilia from three years as a public defender and two years as a judge. She cleared a valley in the mountains of paperwork and began tugging at the plastic shell around her standard lunch—a vending machine package of peanut-butter crackers. She sighed with fatigue, having had enough burglary, prostitution, and assault cases to last a whole week—and it was only Monday. A hearty knock interrupted her wrestling efforts to open her lunch.

"Come in, and bring a shovel," she ordered loudly. She put a corner of the little package between her short, strong teeth and gave a sharp jerk. The door opened and Jake stepped inside, a wicker basket in his arms. Her package ripped open, and crackers flew everywhere.

"Nice to see you, too," he said happily. "Have a nice weekend in Florida?" He kicked the door shut with the heel of his work boot. Vivian distractedly rounded up crackers, thinking that he looked, if possible, even more attractive than ever. His reddish hair was windblown, and his sheepskin coat sat on his wide shoulders as though it were tailor-made. Despite herself, she felt as giddy and flustered.

"Look at my lunch!" she protested weakly. "Get that cracker from under the bookcase over there!"

"That's not lunch, that's parrot food." He settled the basked on the edge of her cluttered desk. "Look here. I thought I'd surprise you. If I'm acting like a stalker, kick me out. Blame Barney Washington—he's the one who got me through security up here to your office. He's a big ol' romantic, that man."

"Jake, I don't do lunch dates . . . "

"This isn't a date. See, I'm not stayin'. I'm just deliverin'."

He quickly set out plastic containers and a single plate. She scowled and spluttered, waving her hands. "What . . . you can't leave all this food here . . . where are you . . . you're not really leaving . . . "

"Yep. Me and Roberto got a meeting with a plumber. Trying to get all the commodes running." He grinned and tipped an invisible hat to her as he backed out of her office.

"Come back, you can't just stuff me and disappear," she yelled. As those words left her mouth she froze. Titters rose from the desks outside her office.

Jake ducked his head around the door frame. "No need to holler. I'll be back later, if you insist."

She narrowed her eyes and hissed at him.

He grinned and left.

ભ • ૭

An hour later she drifted back to court for the afternoon session, drowsy from the effects of fried chicken, homemade biscuits, baked apples with honey, potato salad, and pecan pie. *Thank heavens this robe is so big*, she thought languidly.

"You all right?" Tom asked curiously, as she plopped down at her desk. Callender leaned behind Vivian's back.

"She had a lunchtime visitor," Vivian heard the court secretary whisper. "He brought her a picnic."

"Aw, that's sweet. Did he promise to take her to the fair and walk her home from church on Sunday?"

"Gimme the first case, you cretins," Vivian demanded.

"There he is," Cal whispered loudly.

Tom chuckled. "Well, if isn't Forrest Gump."

Vivian, who'd been absently staring at the docket in

front of her, jerked her head up in time to see Jake ease into the courtroom and settle comfortably onto a back bench. He tipped his head to her.

"Her Honor's got a boyfriend," Tom chanted softly, and Vivian felt her full stomach take a nervous dip.

"And you're about to have a gavel up your . . . nose." She glared at him then pivoted to sear Cal with a look, too. Smiling, they retreated.

Chapter Five

Icy rain turned Atlanta slate-gray outside Vivian's office window. Inside the office, Cal's tears turned Vivian's already bleak mood the same color.

"I love him, Vivian, and he's killing me," Cal said softly, holding her hands over her stricken face. "I can't believe he bought a forty-thousand-dollar motorcycle. He promised he wouldn't buy one until we get our bills in order."

"Tell him v*attene*, baby." Vivian sliced the air with her hand. "Which in what my Italian grandmother used to say. It means, 'So long.'"

"Viv, you don't, you can't understand. When you love someone . . . "

"I haven't always been a dried-up old bag with no romance in my soul."

"I didn't mean that you're heartless. You're just so self-sufficient. You have a thick shell."

"Like a turtle," Vivian told her dryly. "How charming."

"I can't leave him. Divorce is against everything I've ever thought marriage should be."

"So is lying, cheating and bankruptcy. You're being a doormat. If he knows he can walk on you, he'll keep doing it. Men. Bah."

"Is that why you haven't seen Jake Coltrane in a week? You think he considers you an easy touch?"

"I've been busy, that's all."

"Vivian, he's the sweetest man on the face of this earth," she whispered brokenly. "Don't let him get away."

Vivian inhaled with ragged effort. "I know," she admitted just as tearfully. "And he scares me to death. I feel like a squirrel in the middle of traffic. I don't know which way to run."

They were still sniffling when Tom came in. "Isn't there something in your job description about waiting to be asked before you clump into somebody's office?" Vivian demanded in a cranky tone.

"Don't beat me, your majesty, I've brought you some new peasants to work in Forrest Gump's fields."

"I'm going to get you for this," Vivian promised tautly, as she and Cal followed him out the door.

"Hey. It's winter, and the shelters are full. And wait'll you see these three, they'll rip your heart out."

I don't need any more heart-ripping, she thought.

ભ • ૪૦

She saw Jake before he saw her. Shivering in the drizzle that misted her face and dampened her long coat, Vivian gazed through the iron gate and watched him step out of the doorway of one of the upstairs apartments, a heavy tool belt slung over his big shoulder. He pulled the apartment door shut and locked it. Her heart did gymnastics. This man was born to tempt a woman.

Oh, it's good to look at him again, Vivian thought fervently. He wore old gray sweat pants that sculpted themselves to his rangy legs and hard butt. The thick, khaki sweater that covered what appeared to be several layers of flannel shirts made his long torso look even broader than she remembered. She strained for a glimpse of his wind-burned face in profile.

He twisted around and caught sight of her.

"Viv!" he yelled.

The tool belt landed with a thud at his feet. He leaped to the head of the wrought-iron staircase and came down it three steps at a time. Vivian gasped in surprise at the unexpected reception and lost her composure. She backed away from the gate unsteadily, jerking her gloved hands out of her coat pockets. She held her hands in front of her in a *slow-down* gesture, to no avail.

He covered the courtyard in a half-dozen touchdown strides and grabbed the locked gate with both hands, smiling through it at her.

"Viv," he said warmly. The pure delight at seeing her poured into his rich baritone. She nearly melted.

"I came to see you . . . there's some business." He was hurriedly undoing the padlock, and she eyed him nervously. "I need your help."

The lock opened, the gate opened, then he snatched her into his arms.

"Coltrane!" she sputtered, as he swung her around full circle. Vivian's arms had no choice but to go around his neck and hold on for dear life. He stopped, his arms snug around her, and tilted his head back. His smile faded into a serious perusal of her face that sent fingers of sensation down her spine.

"I'm here on business," she said firmly, her voice carefully neutral. "Now please put me down. It's nice to see you again, too."

He continued to hold her and to look up at her. The mist wet his ruddy face and formed tiny droplets on his brows and his lashes; it flattened his hair a littler and gave him an unkempt, vulnerable look that was too tempting for her emotional good.

Vivian tapped his shoulder, refusing to give into the softness that tugged at her heart. "Down, please. There are three pairs of curious eyes watching this whole scene from my car. You're not going to be very happy when you find out what I want."

He set her down gently, his gaze never leaving her stubborn expression. "Viv, I know I musta seemed kind of, uh, too enthusiastic when I sat in your courtroom all afternoon. I just got carried away watching you work."

"Let's just be calm, let's just be friends. I apologize for avoiding you the past week. But I don't 'do' romance well." She straightened her coat awkwardly. "I'm here on business, and not very pleasant business, either, I'm afraid. Like I said, you're not going to be happy when you find out what I need."

Jake hooked his thumbs into the top of his sweatpants and bowed his head thoughtfully. "I'm listening."

"I talked to Roberto. He said you're letting him move into one of the apartments and you gave him some money."

"Enough for him to scrape together a few things. A bed, an old table, a couple of chairs, a fridge, a stove. We scrounged through every salvage shop in town."

"I got you into this. I'll pay you back," Vivian assured him.

"No. He works hard. He's good at carpentry, just like you said. I told him I'd give him what I could." Jake slowly looked over at her car. He cleared his throat. "I see a lot of eyeballs looking back at me."

"They're attached to three people who need jobs and homes. Come on, I'll introduce you."

Jake followed her to the car, right on her heels.

"Outta the way, Tough Stuff."

Like a human forklift, he picked her up and set her aside, ignoring her undignified squeal of surprise. Jake bent forward, rested one hand on the car's roof and the other on his angled hip then swept her passengers with an appraising gaze.

"How do, folks," he said jovially.

"Hi," they chorused back politely. He grinned. They grinned.

"Jake, this is Ray and Fayra Preston." Vivian pointed to the couple. "They're brother and sister, and they're from Bent Switch, Kentucky. They used to work on a farm there."

Jake and Ray nodded to each other again. Ray was in the front passenger seat. Fayra sat in the back beside a smooth-faced, sloe-eyed young man with blond hair.

"Hi, Jake Coltrane," the man said with childlike precision.

"This is Andy Rutledge," Vivian said grimly. "He's been hanging out with Ray and Fayra, and they look after him. I think he's from Cleveland."

"I'm not s-slow," Andy said with great dignity. "No matter what anybody s-says."

"Of course you're not slow," Jake echoed, smiling at him. "You just like to think things over a while, I bet."

"That's r-right, Jake. That's right. You understand!"

"Ray, you and Fayra worked tobacco up in Kentucky?" Jake interrupted, scanning them with friendly eyes.

"You bet," Fayra answered. "Hard work, too, but we were good at it."

"If you worked tobacco, I know you worked hard," he told them. "You need work now?"

"Oh, yes! Yes, we sure do!" they chorused. Jake looked at Andy. "What can you do, son?"
"I'm real good with animals, Jake. And I can do anything anybody shows me how to do!"

"He's a good boy, Mr. Coltrane," Ray added. "All you have to do is guide him a little. He'll work 'til he drops."

Fayra, fortyish and plump, had a pretty, gentle face and expressive eyes that snapped with intelligence. Now she frowned.

"We don't want to be any trouble, and we don't want to go to any shelter with a bunch of heathens. If we can't work for our dinner, we'd rather starve."

"Nobody gets handouts around here," Jake said cheerfully. "They get as much as I can pay, for as much as they can work."

Vivian watched her three passengers brighten. She touched Jake's arm. "I can help with expenses—"

"I don't need any handouts," he said primly. "You go tell Roberto he's got new neighbors. Go on, now." He poked her shoulder playfully. "Go. Shoo."

"Go on, Viv," Andy repeated solemnly. "We'll stay with Jake. He'll take care of us. What do we do first, Jake?"

"I think we ought to—" Vivian tried.

"Andy, you go with Viv. Ray and Fayra and me will unload y'all's things. Viv, go on now, tell Roberto what's goin' on."

"I . . . oh . . . okay," she muttered. She felt unnecessary, a fifth wheel, a squeaky and abrasive fifth wheel. "Everything will be fine. Y'all can quit worrying. I've never let anybody down and I guarantee you—"

"Nobody's worried, Viv," Jake said cheerfully. "You just relax, too."

"No one even noticed that she looked forlorn, because they were all busy getting out of the car. Jake joked over the trunk full of bedrolls and burlap bags, oblivious to her. Her head down and her eyes brooding, she walked away.

愉 • 愉

Over the course of the two busy hours that followed. Jake grew more and more worried about her. She didn't make wisecracks, she didn't give him the pert, scolding looks he had already grown to cherish, and she didn't boss anyone around. She simply found little chores to do and did them quietly, her black-haired head bent and her hazel eyes dull.

He gave her one of his shirts to wear over her suit, and she went to work in the apartment next to Roberto's, sweeping out the empty bedrooms, dusting.

Jake stole looks at her; if only she cared about him the way he cared about her.

He caught Vivian looking at him. His stomach drifted down around his knees and stayed there. She had such a frail, sad, little-girl expression on her face that he almost forgot how snippy she'd been earlier.

They stood staring at each other in an empty bedroom. Before Jake could move toward her, Roberto swaggered into the room and allowed that he was going to give his bed to Fayra, if Jake thought that was a good idea.

"We'll buy some more beds," Vivian said immediately, drawing her gaze away from Jake's. "And some basic furniture." She gestured at Roberto. "Come on. We'll browse the Goodwill store first then check out the offerings at the Freight Overstock outlet." To Jake she said, "Can we take your truck?"

She had extra money and he didn't, so he handed

60

her his truck keys. He and she walked into the hallway, Roberto trailing along. Fayra and Andy stopped dusting the walls and smiled shyly.

"This is a wonderful place, Jake," Fayra told him, her eyes gleaming with tears. "We'll work for our room and board harder than anybody you've ever seen."

"You've already put in a week's worth of work," he replied. "Slow down."

Smiling, Jake looked over at Vivian. His smile died. Her eyes were downcast. She removed his work shirt and tossed it haphazardly on a small crate Roberto had procured as a hallway table then she cleared her throat and went into the kitchen to retrieve her purse and coat from a counter.

"Hey!" Roberto exclaimed, as he grabbed his own coat. "You guys can't guess where me and Viv are goin'! Jake's lettin' us take the truck to buy some mattresses and some other stuff to make the place a regular palace for everybody!"

"Thank you, Jake," Andy said in worshipping awe, "for buying us some stuff. Nobody has ever been so good to us as you have."

"I'm not the one to thank," Jake began quickly.

"Mr. Coltrane, we'll sure earn this," Ray interjected, pumping Jake's hand. Jake looked down at the serious and wizened face so much older than Fayra's and knew Ray was telling the truth.

"God bless you," Fayra murmured, nearly crying. "We never knew this old world had so much goodness in it before we met you."

Jake glanced up in time to see a strangled expression cross Vivian's face. Her eyes on Fayra, she gave a light, almost imperceptible nod of agreement. Jake's broad chest almost burst with emotion.

"Now y'all, just turn yourselves around and thank the right person," he started, but Vivian shook her head and hurried out the door before he could finish.

☙ • ❧

Midnight came and went before they finished setting up the three twin-sized bed frames complete with top quality mattresses and box springs. Jake couldn't believe the amount of money Vivian had spent. She'd bought sheets, pillows, and blankets. She'd bought a stove and kitchen utensils. She'd even bought a small television set. On the way back, she'd directed Roberto to stop at a grocery store. While everyone else was putting the groceries away, Jake drew Roberto into the living room.

"How much?" he demanded. "Gimme the total." Roberto's eyes went wide. He held up two fingers. "Two thousand?" Jake asked.

"Yeah, man, two thousand." Roberto lowered his voice to a whisper. "You don't understand the Judge. She doesn't know how to let other people take care of her. She gets nervous when anybody else takes charge. Her husband was a dick, man. He used to boss her around, give her orders, run the whole show. And then when he left her, he made it sound like she deserved it."

"Oh, my Lord," Jake said slowly. He rubbed his forehead in dismay. "I guess I look like another take-charge bullshit artist to her."

"Yes, I'm afraid so."

"I'll take care of it. Don't tell her you told me, Roberto."

"Oh, I won't! She'd kill me."

Jake ambled into the kitchen with Roberto behind him.

"Everybody settled for the night?" he asked pleasantly. They were putting the last groceries away. Secluded in one corner, Vivian put a final can of turnip greens into a cabinet. She fumbled it, dropped it on the counter, then grabbed it with a weary hand.

"We're settled, Jake," Fayra replied. She turned from the stove and held up a frying pan. "I'm going to fix some dinner for these fellows. You and Vivian want to stay?"

"Thank you ma'am, but I need to talk to Viv upstairs," Jake answered. Vivian swung around and looked at him in dull surprise. "Will you get your things and come upstairs a minute?" he asked.

"Sure."

Once inside his apartment, he pointed her toward the living room. "How about a shot of Jack Daniels?"

"I'll take it," she mumbled, as he switched on an old floor lamp with a fringed shade. His living room looked like a museum for 1940's furniture. The couch and chairs were upholstered in a quaint, fading flower print. The coffee table was heavy and ornate, scarred with moisture rings and little nicks. A massive roll top desk dominated one wall, and plain, unpainted bookshelves covered another. The shelves were filled with horticulture and veterinary books. A white-brick fireplace angled across one corner of the room.

"What do you want with your bourbon, Viv?"

"What are you having?"

"I drink my bourbon straight."

"Well . . . so do I."

Jake, who had knelt in front of the fireplace to arrange fresh wood, twisted around to stare at her. He chuckled ruefully, goaded a steady little kindling fire under the logs, and went to the kitchen shaking his head. A minute later, he came back with a bottle and two shot glasses full of bourbon, which he set on the coffee table. He handed her a glass and sat down a comfortable distance from her on the couch. He held his glass aloft, and she followed suit.

"Here's to closin' spaces," Jake said softly. Vivian hesitated, then clinked her glass with his. Jake tossed the amber liquid down in one swallow, grimaced slightly, and set his glass on the table. "Sometimes that's the best way to drink it," he began, "but you'd better sip—"

She gulped her drink. Her face perfectly composed, she thumped her glass down.

"Viv! I'm a lot bigger than you are. You can't match me drink for drink."

"Try me."

He poured them both another shot. Vivian held her glass up. "An apology," she said quietly. "I've been a pain. You're a good guy."

"Why, thank you, darlin'," he answered in a distracted voice, watching as she swallowed her second shot of bourbon. He drank his, and it sprinted warmly through his veins. Jake blinked several times, rapidly. She looked at him with her head tilted to one side and a cocky expression on her face. Jake decided that his pride was at stake. "Is this a challenge?" he asked jauntily, his eyes tight on hers.

In answer, one corner of her mouth crooked up, and she poured them another drink. They clicked the glasses together a little harder than before.

"Here's to finding out which one of us is the boss in this twosome," she told him with narrowed eyes.

"Ah-hah. I see where this is headin'."

They sat there a minute, just staring at each other,

then polished off another round. This time they set down their glasses in unison. Hers rattled as she let go it, and his eyes flew to her unsteady hand.

"You lose," he said huskily. "Enough of this."

"No!" She grabbed the Jack Daniels. With just as much stubbornness, he took the bottle away from her, capped it, and stood up. "Let's call it a draw."

He turned on his heel, walked toward the kitchen slowly, his back straight and almost made it all the way out the double doors before he bumped into one of them.

"I win," she called.

"No way," he called back. "I meant to hit that door."

When he returned, she had gone to stand in the deep shadows by a window. He saw her slumped shoulders and lowered head, and his heart twisted. He crossed the dimly lit room and took her arm.

"Would you come on over here and sit down?" he asked gently. "I've got things to say to you."

With a grim look, she sidled over to the couch. She settled on one end of the flowery cushions and stared morosely into space.

He sat down within arm's reach.

"Look here, Viv, I want to tell you somethin'. But first, can I . . . " He nodded at her hands.

"Give me a manicure?" she supplied drily.

"Hold your hands."

She held them out. "On loan."

He wound his fingers between hers and squeezed gently. "I just want to tell you that what you've done for those four people downstairs is the best, the kindest thing I've ever seen in my life."

"It's part of my job. I'm all about justice."

"I don't think it's that simple."

"It is, to me."

"You've got a heart the size of a harvest moon," he told her gruffly. Her eyes met his and clung. "I feel so humble when I look at all the good you do. I watched you last week in court and I thought, 'She really cares about people.' I need for you to care about *me*. I need you. I don't mean to come on too strong; I'm not trying to control you. I'm just a . . . a bull in a china shop when it comes to small talk. I can't do it. I just . . . I just say what I think. It's a country-boy curse."

She smiled tentatively. "I'm trying to get used to it."

"I won't make another move without your absolute go-ahead. Nothing. Not even a wink. Not even a half-a-wink." He made a dramatic and comical show of almost-winking.

Vivian gave a throaty laugh then slid close to him and put her arms around his neck. Jake suddenly found himself surrounded by the scent of her and then the taste of her as she pressed her mouth to his. Her hands slid down his chest, then around his back and down the flexed curve of his spine. Jake gasped into her mouth as her hands curved along the sides of his hips and the outsides of his thighs. Vivian made a ragged sound and quickly put her hands on his chest.

She tipped her head back, her eyes half-closed and her face flushed. "If you push me too hard, I'll push back. Fair warning?"

He looked at her breathlessly, wanting her so badly that his whole body ached. "Tell me what part you want pushed first."

"Surprise me."

His fingers trembled as he wound them into the scarf knotted at her throat. He pulled its bow undone.

She kept her gaze on his eyes as his fingers slid down the center of her blouse, pressing lightly on the cool material until they indented it between her breasts.

Her chest swelled invitingly against his fingers. A shudder ran through him, and he pulled his hand away from her. He touched her cheek and looked pensively down into her vulnerable eyes.

Vivian pressed herself to him quickly and began undoing his shirt. Their legs tangled as she gave him a small push backward on the couch. Her hands slipped inside the worn material and caressed his chest with eager movements that tugged at the curly hair. Jake groaned and grabbed her wrists.

"I don't want to do it this way," he said raggedly.

Vivian stiffened at the rebuke in his voice as it seeped through her hazy thoughts. "I don't understand."

She tried to pull away, but he only held her tighter. "Where are you going, girl?""Either I keep running away from you or I make you want to run from me. You're confusing me."

"Did I say I want to run from you?" he demanded gently. "But you're drunk. I don't want you to wake up in the morning looking at me like I'm a hangover you want to forget."

She started to say something else, but her lips froze on the words. She swayed a little, blinking owlishly. "Are you for real?"

He leaned his forehead against hers. "So real I could kick myself for playin' fair."

"I'm not too drunk to make a decision about sex."

"You had to get drunk to kiss me."

"Not a bad way to jump-start things. I may be rusty, but I'm fast."

"Viv, that's the point. Let's make this special. I've had enough hook-ups and disappointments and reckless failures. So have you. Let's take it slow."

For an uncertain moment, he waited for her response.

"If my Pop were still alive," she said finally, her voice warm, "I think he'd invite you over for dinner, and he'd make his fancy spaghetti sauce for you. With extra olive oil He never invited *any* of my boyfriends over for his extra-olive-oil spaghetti."

"Good. I'd be honored to eat spaghetti your daddy made." He looked at her gently. "Think you're ready to let me share some of that *space* of yours?" he asked. A hint of a smile touched his mouth.

Vivian slowly put her head on his shoulder then settled into a comfortable position in his arms. Jake sighed. "We're a good pair, Viv," he whispered. "Like ham and grits."

"Like ham and spaghetti," she whispered back.

Chapter Six

Vivian hurried around her condo, trying to make its eclectic clutter look neat. She was in the midst of rearranging the army of sauce pans that hung on brass hooks over her stove when the doorbell chimed.

"Dammit, Jake, you're on time!"

She shoved two saucepans into the white cabinet nearby and ran to the guest bath to peer at herself in the mirror. "You better like this outfit," she muttered, smoothing her hands over her soft, gray sweater interwoven with glittering silver. "I don't twinkle for just *any* man." She wore loose, gray, brushed-denim trousers with the sweater, and gray leather flats. She preferred to think of all that gray as *pewter*, and considered it elegant.

"Well, it's about time," she began, swinging the door open. "*Te presento la casa mia.* Welcome to my home for your first visit . . . Jake?"

He stood awkwardly on the brick doorstep—she thought it was him, at least. It could have been a philodendron with long legs. Two huge plants in clay pots hid his handsome face and torso.

"I already made a salad," she quipped, taking one of the pots. He laughed, the sound so robust that it seemed to warm the icy air that swept in the open door around him. He stepped inside, juggled the remaining plant, and leaned toward her. After a moment's hesitation, she gave him a quick, soft kiss. Their plants intertwined. Vivian smiled as she untangled the philodendron tendrils.

"I asked Roberto what I could bring you, and he said you like plants," Jake explained.

Vivian nodded, then eyed the plants distractedly and Jake seriously as she took his coat. He did more for jeans and cotton work shirts than any other man on earth. "You're very thoughtful. Let's put them on my sun porch. Then I'll play Barefoot Contessa."

"Who?"

"She's a chef on the Food Network."

"With bare feet?"

She shut the door and guided him forward, one hand on his shoulder. "Nevermind."

He followed her through the living room to a glassed-in porch filled with white wicker furniture and colorful Indian rugs. And plants. Dozens of them. All kinds—hanging, drooping, standing, menacing the furniture, some of them plastered against the windows as if they wanted out. Jake stopped at the entrance and gazed at them in despair.

"Bringin' you more plants is like throwin' alligator eggs into a swamp," he moaned. "I should have got you somethin' else."

"Oh, I love plants. Two more will be just terrific." She lowered his gift-plants into one of the last clear spots. "You boys behave there, now." Vivian squatted beside them and stroked their leaves. "Don't make any trouble, or I'll sic the cacti on you. I'll water you tomorrow, after you've settled in and relaxed."

When she stood up, Jake was smiling at her so rapturously that she blushed. "What'sa matter?" she grumbled. "You're a farmer. Don't you believe in talking to plants?"

"Not like they're gonna talk back." He held out his arms. "Come here and gimme a hug, you little turnip green."

"No, no, no. I have to go check the raviolli."

"Chicken."

"No, beef," she countered, trying to slide by him without touching.

"There you go, runnin' off to that safe little place you keep inside somewhere."

"I'm only seductive when I drink Jack Daniels."

"You need to learn to snuggle, Viv. Just cause we took a vow of chastity doesn't mean we can't giggle and tickle."

She looked up at him wistfully. "I was raised to be totally good or totally bad. I don't understand this odd thing called courtship on your planet, stranger."

He smiled. "Why are we standin' here weighin' the world when we could be havin' a good time? Let's stop all this serious talk. It makes my head hurt."

"Mine, too," Vivian said firmly. "Come on, I have to continue your education in Italian cuisine."

They walked back into the living room. Soft jazz spilled out of the iPod berthed atop speakers in one corner. A flat-screen TV dominated one wall. Jake held one hand out to test the cozy warmth of the fake logs that crackled in her faux fireplace.

"You build a great fire for a city girl. I'm impressed. Who knew ceramic oak kindling could catch a flame so well. Hope the ravioli weren't baked in a kiln."

"You have to learn to appreciate our differences," Vivian retorted, but she smiled. "And that's why I have a surprise for you after dinner."

ଓ • ଓ

He looked awkward sitting on her overstuffed

white couch in the dim light of the fire and the glow of one soft lamp in a distant corner. Vivian sat down on the hearth across from him and sipped her after-dinner coffee as she studied him.

"Nice place you got here," he said politely.

"You look like—" she gave him a thoughtful frown—"like a Norman Rockwell character who wandered into the wrong painting."

"I feel like one."

He looked at her white recliner and white couch, her sleek brass lamps and rare law books, her collection of ceramic dragons, her stacks of medieval fantasy novels, and—with a satisfied smile, as if he'd found some friends—at her country-quilt throw pillows. Vivian set her cup down on the gleaming glass coffee table between them and rubbed her hands together briskly.

"I'll be back in a second. I told you about the surprise for tonight."

"I don't like that look in your eyes, Viv."

Chuckling softly, she left the room. When she came back ten minutes later, she still wore her shimmering sweater, but she'd traded her slacks for a black leather miniskirt and lacy white hose. Black ankle boots with slender heels now replaced her flats.

He stood up to hide his arousal. "And what'd you do to your hair?"

"I just fluffed it up and put some hair spray in it," she answered patiently.

"What are you holdin' behind your back?"

"Stop looking at me like I just grew fangs. Bend over so I can work on your hair."

"Well . . . sure."

When he bowed his head to her she whipped out a

can of spray gel. Quickly she formed his short, dense and wavy red hair into a spiky masterpiece. "There. Just enough to be edgy; not so much it says 'boy band.'"

"My hair is protestin', either way."

They stared at each other in portentous silence.

"Hair can't talk," she deadpanned.

"Mine is too upset to say a word," he countered.

ଓ • ଞ

The music was loud and had no melody, the crowd was pierced and tattooed, and the drinks came in plastic mugs with BITE ME stenciled on their sides.

"Just like Vacation Bible School," Jake yelled over the clang of amped-up guitars.

He kept his hand under Vivian's elbow in his usual gentlemanly way as they angled through tables looking for a place to sit in throbbing darkness. A drunk with plugs the size of lug nuts in his ear lobes screamed at Viv, "YOU MAKE ME WANT TO TOUCH MYSELF."

Jake calmly raised a big, callused hand, intending to clamp it over his face and shove his head down inside his rib cage. Vivian grabbed Jake's arm just in time. The drunk turned even paler than his white make-up and scurried away.

They finally found a table and sat down. Vivian studied Jake anxiously. This nightclub was considered one of the best alternative-music venues in the South. Despite the grungy warehouse setting in an industrial part of the city, the club had a good reputation among music critics, and it drew a diverse crowd. About half the clubbers looked as if they'd just come from a sale at Pottery Barn. Not exactly a wild group.

She watched Jake watch the action. He leaned toward her and yelled, "I've seen rougher crowds at

Garth Brooks concerts."

She laughed. They ordered drinks—beer for her, straight bourbon for him. And he continued his examination of the place.

An elegant, tall brunette with perfect makeup and a broad-shouldered figure outlined by a gorgeous black jumpsuit sidled up to their table and smiled at Jake. He stood politely.

"Can I ask him to dance?" the woman asked Vivian in a throaty voice.

Vivian looked closely at the beautiful creature trying to whisk Jake away. She rose languidly and draped an arm atop Jake's broad shoulder. "Thank you, baby, but I just go sick crazy when I see him with another girl."

The woman shrugged and glided away. Jake stared after her, his mouth open. Vivian elbowed him. "Sit down, Coltrane. That was a guy."

He sank into the chair and turned to look at her. His eyes filled with a pleased glow. "You really didn't want me to dance with her? With him? I mean, it matters to you if I dance with another . . . well, someone who looks like a woman?"

She looked furtive, rolled her eyes, *tsked,* then tossed up a hand. "Okay. You caught me. Yeah."

"I shoulda danced with him. Just to impress you. To prove I fit in here."

A tender fire began to burn inside Vivian. "I don't want you to fit in here."

"But then why . . . "

"I'm a jerk. I wanted to impress *you* with my sophisticated tastes." She nodded toward the weirdness around them. "But this isn't for me, either."

The smile seemed to start somewhere inside his

chest and grow out of him until it transformed his face. Vivian caught her breath at the look in his eyes. He took her hands and brought each one to his lips for generous kisses. Vivian's eyelids fluttered down to half-mast and her mouth parted in a sigh.

Jake's eyes gleamed. "You and me, we aren't from such different worlds. I bet you'd be right at home up in Tuna Creek."

"Let's not get carried away."

"Fair trade, darlin'. Now it's my turn to educate *you*."

"Uh-oh," she said dryly. "I don't know…"

"Don't go hollerin' about your space, now. I'm gonna go visit my Aunt Vanessa next weekend—go up on Saturday and stay overnight. Why don't you come along?"

Vivian thought for a second, her instincts warning her that a visit to Aunt Vanessa and Tuna Creek would be another turning point in this relationship—either toward dangerous intimacy or toward the harsh reality that things would never work.

She had to know.

"All right." She raised her chin. "It's a date."

He leaped up from the chair. "I can't sit still, darlin'! Let's dance!"

Vivian tilted her head toward the floor crowded with people slamming and bouncing around.

"You want to do *that*?"

"No! I want to dance!"

She laughed until her sides hurt. In the meantime he pulled her gently into his arms. What he called dancing, as it turned out, involved holding her with her head on his chest and his rough chin resting against her widow's peak. It was slow dancing, totally inappropriate considering the music and the fact that everyone else was funking out. Jake lowered his head and let his lips brush her ear.

"Do you mind my kind of dancin'?"

Vivian turned her face up to the warm hollow of his throat and planted a kiss there.

"I love it."

And I'm beginning to love you, she added silently.

Chapter Seven

She became aware of bright morning sun all around her and a bear snapping at the hem of her judicial robes as she drove a tractor that looked oddly like her Prius through a field of corn. She gave the bear a karate chop, and it laughed. Vivian's eyes flew open.

"Back! Back!" she gasped, jerking upright.

"What's the matter?" Jake asked. Wild-eyed and ruffled, Vivian glanced vaguely at the highway flashing past with winter-brown mountains in the distance. She looked at him blankly.

"A bear was after me in Tuna Creek!"

He smiled, chuckled softly, and took one hand off his truck's steering wheel to stroke her disheveled hair into place. His hand settled along her cheek, his fingertips feather-light and soothing.

"Go back to snoozin'. Well be at Aunt Vanessa's about lunchtime."

"Uhmmm." A week of hectic court during the day and they mayor's committee on midtown crime at night had kept her contact with Jake to one lunch and five late-night telephone conversations. "Where are we?"

"Oh, somewhere northeast of Nashville and west of Soddy-Daisy."

"And Soddy-Daisy is where?"

"South of Shoe Bin and east of Catterwaul."

She stared at his amused profile. "Gee, freakin' thanks."

He laughed.

Vivian settled back on the truck's seat. "So we're getting into the blank part of the Tennessee state map. I'm sorry I slept so long. I haven't seen you all week, and I didn't mean to keel over as soon as I got in the truck. But it was five a.m."

"*Sssh.*" He guided her head back to his shoulder, where she had slept cozily for almost three hours. "I like hearin' you breathe. And you make cute little sounds, like a kitten."

"A city kitten. Do you think I'm dressed right?" She looked from his standard outfit—heavy flannel shirt, jeans, work boots, and sheepskin jacket—to hers. Vivian wore a short, unstructured tweed coat over loose tan trousers, and a sweater splashed with abstract earth-tone images. Chestnut-brown boots with high heels finished the outfit, along with the brown fedora she'd tucked on top of the truck's faded dashboard.

Jake glanced at her out of the corner of his eye and smiled tentatively. "You're . . . fine. I like your clothes real well."

"Aren't you sleepy? Do you want me to drive?"

"Nah, morning's my best time. I feel great when I get up before dawn. On the farm, I'd have fifty head milked by seven a.m. every day."

"Well, if you're just doing their heads, of *course* you can work that fast."

His laughter mingled with the crisp sunshine to wrap her in unaccustomed contentment. Jake made her feel that everything had a calm purpose in life, that the world didn't need as much supervision as she'd always thought.

She fell asleep again on his shoulder, listening to him hum along with a bluegrass gospel song pouring from the truck's satellite radio feed. In Jake's world, no contrast seemed ironic, and contentment simmered on the magic of the moment.

C♀ • ℰ⅁

Aunt Vanessa's blue, two-story farmhouse sat snuggly in a wooded hollow, surrounded by the winter skeletons of old fruit trees and giant oaks. A dozen fat chickens scurried out of the front yard as they drove up. Vivian opened the truck door and was immediately surrounded by a mountain silence she found almost eerie. Smoke rose from a stone chimney on the house. A small barn with a peaked roof sat a hundred yards away, behind a split-rail fence that curved on either side into the woods. Vivian inhaled aromatic, smoke-tinted air.

Abruptly, Aunt Vanessa burst out of her clapboard farmhouse with a white sweater flapping around her wiry body and her arms thrown out to Jake.

"My little honey, come give Aunt Vanny a kiss!"

"You got it, darlin'!"

Jake loped up to her, and Vivian followed slowly. She stopped behind him and watched with a smile as Jake swept the small, white-haired woman into his arms and swung her around. Aunt Vanessa pounded his broad back with work-gnarled hands, giggling like a child. He put her down gently.

"Aunt Vanny, you're still one of the prettiest girls in Tuna Creek."

"No, no, Lord, let me see your intended!"

Vivian didn't quite know what to say to that remark—his *intended?*—so she just smiled awkwardly. Aunt Vanessa's Coltrane eyes—warm and blue—scanned her from toe to head and seemed to approve.

"Can Aunt Vanny get a hug from you too, darlin'?"

Before Vivian could answer she found herself being bear-hugged by a fellow short person who smelled of lilac talc and butter. Vivian hugged back uncomfortably. Apparently, the Coltranes never considered anyone a stranger. They grinned at each other. "Oh, this is a special day! Jacob, you've got such a pretty fiancée!"

As Aunt Vanny tugged Vivian up a fieldstone path to the house, Vivian gave Jake a sharply inquiring look, to which he cleared his throat and shook his head in mute denial.

෪ • ൫

He had no chance to explain until two hours later. They sat in Aunt Vanessa's living room, sipping hot cups of tea thick with fresh cream while Vivian admired antique chairs and hand-embroidered pillows. Aunt Vanessa excused herself to take a blood-pressure pill. As soon as she left the room, Jake slid close to Vivian on the couch.

"I didn't tell her we're engaged. She frets all the time about me bein' alone, and she just got carried away when she heard you were comin'. I'll tell her the truth when she gets back."

"I can see that your marital status means a lot to her. Don't ruin her weekend, just tell her later."

A mischievous glint came in his eyes. "So you *like* the idea?"

"Beat it," she ordered, and pointed to an opposing chair.

Chuckling, he moved.

෪ • ൫

Vivian and Aunt Vanny sat on the back porch after lunch, wrapped in quilts and sipping mugs of hot tea, while Jake repaired a light fixture in the small shed that housed Aunt Vanny's hatchback.

"Let's talk turkey," the older woman said. She reached under her quilt and pulled out a small bottle of bourbon. "Wild Turkey." As Vivian gaped at her, Aunt Vanny dosed Vivian's tea with the liquor, then doctored her own mug.

Aunt Vanny hid the bottle in her quilt again then lifted her mug. "Here's to skunks and drunks and men with plenty of junk in their trunks."

Vivian nearly fell over laughing. Then she clicked her mug to Aunt Vanny's. Jake's aunt nodded her approval. They downed a hearty swallow or two. When the bourbon loosened their tongues, Aunt Vanny asked quietly, "So, what do you want to know about him?"

Vivian cupped both hands around her warm mug. "He doesn't say much about his parents. What's the story?"

"His daddy died when Jake was just a baby. His mama ran the dairy well enough but partied with the wrong men, drugs, drink, and so forth. Jake spent more time here with me than with her. He tried his best to take care of her, but she pretty much broke his heart. She died, drunk, in her car, when he was seventeen. He buckled down to run the dairy and keep the family farm. The boy has never gotten many lucky breaks, and he's never had it easy. But he doesn't complain."

Aunt Vanny pinned her with a calm stare. "Now, girl, you tell me what your intentions are. Because he deserves the very best, and he sure seems to think you're it."

Vivian sat in silence for a moment. "No. I'm not good enough for him."

"Oh? How so?"

"I'm not unselfish enough. I'm not family-oriented

enough. I'm a loner. And I'm a pain."

"Let me tell *you*, Miss Viv, he's had plenty of women after him, and the one marriage that wasn't good for him, but I've never seen him look as happy as he looks with you. You've gotten to him in a way that's special. Can you tell me why that's so? I mean, *he's* told me what you do for people, but I'd like to hear your opinion."

"He says it impresses him that I try to take care of people. But it's not my choice . . . it's bred in me, it's who I am. I'm the daughter of a cop. My mother died when I and my brother were small. Our father raised us with the help of our grandmothers. He really cared about people. He died on the job, when I was twelve, shot by a drug dealer. I decided then that I'd go into law. And that I'd try to make a difference in the world."

"That 'difference' doesn't include a husband and children, honey?"

"I thought it did. But my marriage was short and miserable. I don't trust my judgment anymore, where men are concerned."

"Well, I sure do envy you that luxury."

I looked at her warily. "What do you mean?"

"I've been married three times. First husband? Twenty years. Died of kidney problems. I was thirty-seven. We never got pregnant. Second husband? Three years. I miscarried twice. He died of a heart attack. He was only forty-one. Third husband? Five years. We had a baby but it didn't survive a week. And him? He died of a lung infection."

"Aunt Vanny, I'm sorry."

"Don't be sorry. I loved and loved and loved. I'm not too old to love again, if I find the right man."

Vivian sat back in her chair, musing. "I don't know

if I'm that brave."

Aunt Vanny hoisted her bourbon-infused tea. "What takes more courage: loneliness or loss?"

Vivian couldn't answer her.

◌ • ◌

At Aunt Vanny's urging, Jake drove Vivian into Tuna Creek that afternoon for a tour. They rumbled down a tree-lined main street straight out of Mayberry. Pickup trucks dominated the car herd, nosing up to the sidewalks with muddy fenders and I SUPPORT THE SECOND AMENDMENT bumper stickers. Jake parked in front of Tuna Creek Medicinals and Soda Fountain.

"Come on, I'll buy you a cherry Coke, made with coke syrup and real cherry juice and everything," Jake said.

"I might faint from the sugar rush. I'm addicted to artificial sweetener." Vivian suddenly realized she was tapping the truck's floorboard in happy rhythm to a Merle Haggard song on the radio. She stared at her foot as if it had taken on a life of its own. "By the way, I'm overdue for my twice-daily Starbucks fix."

Jake snorted.

"No Starbucks?"

He *harummphed* and busied himself tucking his tractor cap atop the dash. "Caffeine addict."

His tone was teasing so she jibed back: "Decaffinated redneck."

"Hah."

"Okay, what kind of fast food places *do* you have here?"

"Well, there's uh . . . " He turned the truck at the next stop sign and pointed as they closed the distance between themselves and a tiny building with a neon sign of a dancing cow wearing a sundress. "There's the Dairy Dip."

The truck rolled to a stop and Vivian started at the ramshackle place with a handwritten menu in the window. "How long ago was the building condemned?"

"Hey. It's a historic site."

"Preserved in ancient layers of dirt and Crisco." She turned amused eyes on him and saw his brow furrowing. She squeezed his arm. "Ignore me. I'm a condescending snitwad."

His eyes glittered with restored happiness, and he popped the truck into gear again. They rolled past a row of shops nestled side by side behind plank sidewalks. "Cute," she said gamely.

"Wanta go meet some of my friends?" Jake asked.

"Absolutely."

"They usually get together at their watering hole on Saturday afternoons."

"Ah hah. I love cozy little pubs and pool halls."

"Well, that's not it, exactly."

"What do you mean, 'Not exactly?'"

What he meant was Burley's Seed and Feed, a weathered place that had once been the town train depot. It still looked more or less like a depot outside, but the only trains that came by these days were slow-moving freights that, like the rest of the world, didn't take time to stop in Tuna Creek.

Jake steered her up a loading ramp and through a scarred door. A little bell attached to the door announced their arrival to a half-dozen men and women of varying ages who were parked around a pot-bellied stove with their work boots crossed dangerously close to its hot sides. Vivian inhaled the sweet scents of feed, livestock gear, hardware, seeds, and hundreds of other items packed onto rows of shelves separated by narrow aisles. All the men stood politely as she approached. The women chorused hearty hellos and pulled another pair of rump-sprung lawn chairs into the circle. One reached into a cooler and handed her a cold can of beer dripping icewater.

The men grinned at Jake and took turns clasping his hand. The women hugged him and then hugged Vivian. Jake introduced her and wasn't surprised when she stuck her hand out to each man just as normally as he had. Young Ben Talbert shook it without obvious shock; Old Ben Talbert took a startled moment to wipe his hand on his overalls before he tried this unusual man-woman greeting.

Emma Burley, a progressive businesswoman type, guffawed at the old man's attitude and shook Vivian's hand crisply. The blond and crew-cut Braxton brothers—Leon, Ed, and Palmer—managed with shy smiles. Everyone studied her with open fascination. *Like I'm a new breed of cow Jake bought*, she thought wryly.

Jake popped a beer for himself and held Vivian's lawn chair while she sat down. Then he settled in the chair beside hers and sighed happily. *This is where he belongs, this is where he feels at home*, Vivian noted.

Leon Braxton peered at her. "Jake's aunt told us all about you bein' a judge. I've never seen a judge as young as you. How do you scare anybody?"

"Hey," Jake warned.

"No insult intended."

Vivian waved off the remark with a jovial hand. "City court's pretty basic. The meat and potatoes of the justice system. Lots of misdemeanors and petty crime. I was a public defender for about five years before I was offered the position."

"Don't let her looks fool you," Jake put in. "Y'all should see her courtroom face. I've seen her go all Tony Soprano on folks. I call it her 'mob boss eyes.'" He hesitated and glanced at Vivian. "No insult to your people."

"None taken."

Leon persisted, "Why, if we had woman judge up here, I reckon we'd get away with just about anything."

Vivianshrugged, but Jake growled, "Who says a woman can't be as tough and smart as a man?"

The women hooted an nodded while the men shuffled their feet and suppressed smiles.

"Don't pay any attention to Jake," Vivian said diplomatically. "He just happens to be the president of my fan club."

A small boy, bundled up in jeans and an army jacket, banged the door open and stepped inside. A big, shaggy, mixed-breed dog followed him, tail wagging.

"Hey, Tobie," Emma called. "How'd Hagrid do at the 4-H show? Did he win any ribbons on the obstacle course?"

Tobie sighed as the big dog flopped down by his feet. "Nope. He knocked over two of the jumps and hiked his leg on the tunnel tube. Hey, Jake!"

Jake spread and arm and the boy bounded inside it for a hug. Grinning, jake introduced him to Vivian. Tobie tipped his child-sized tractor cap to her. "Aunt Vanny told my mama about you. You gonna marry Jake?"

"Here's ten dollars," Jake interjected hurriedly, pulling a bill from his jean's pocket. "How about you and Hagrid trot down to the Pick n' Go and bring us back some tater chips? And get yourself a candy bar."

"Thanks, dude!" Tobie hit the door running, with Hagrid galloping on his heels. Jake's face was as red as the red plaid in his shirt. Vivian decided to be magnanimous and change the subject.

"I had a dog when I was growing up. I named him 'Democrat.'"

Silence. Everyone looked at the floor. The air prickled. Palmer Braxton snorted. "Poor little dog."

Old Ben Talbert announced, "Might as well name a dog, 'Satan.'"

"Or 'Hitler,'" one of the women said.

Vivian's hackles rose, but she kept her voice light. "Or even worse: 'Reagan.'"

Eyes flashed. Smiles froze. Jake urgently made a 'Time out' T with his hands. But Emma laughed loudly, breaking the tension. "Y'all are all about to step in a big pile of politics." She gave Vivian a look of gracious warning. "Leave their beehive alone . . . and you—" she jabbed a finger at the others—"stick a sock in it."

The group sighed and shrugged.

Emma smiled. "Don't take their big talk too seriously. They may buzz at you for being a Democrat, but about half of them voted for Obama."

"Not me," Leon Braxton said loudly. "He's a Muslim socialist."

That produced groans and head-shaking from half the group but hearty nods from the other half.

Vivian chewed her lip. *Keep quiet, zip it, don't say another word.*

Leon added, "You watch. He'll outlaw barbecue pork and take away our guns and make our kids read the Koran." Leon pointed at her. "Because you crazy liberals voted him into office."

Vivian sputtered. Jake stood up, his jaw tight.

"Come on, darlin', let's get outta here." He slipped into a heavier accent and hometown grammar. "This bunch ain't got nothing better to do than play poker this afternoon, and we'd prob'ly just fall asleep watchin' the wild excitement of *that*."

"Poker?" Vivian said carefully. "If you wouldn't mind a heathen liberal joining the game, I play poker a little."

Jake groaned silently as the group welcomed her behind thin-lipped smiles. They were poker sharks. They played penny-ante games but those pennies added up. They'd gleefully wipe Vivian out.

"Viv, they're pretty serious hands . . . "

His voice faded as she turned her face up to him and gave him a reassuring wink.

Yep. Mob boss eyes.

ભ • ૭

A few hours later, Vivian slid into Jake's truck with a satisfied smile. He settled into the driver's seat, his expression restrained, and started the motor.

"Are you mad at me for punking them?" she asked suddenly, studying his hard-set mouth.

He shook his head. "Sssh. They're watchin' out the windows. I'm trying to be neutral, at least as long as we're on public display."

He drove out of the feedstore's lot. Then he whipped the truck around a corner and pulled into an alley. Vivian gazed at him worriedly as he gripped the steering wheel hard and rested his forehead on it. He began laughing.

He laughed so hard he wasn't even producing a sound. He pounded the steering wheel with one fist. Finally, a deep roar broke free.

"I swear . . . every time you won another hand their

88

mouths fell open a little wider. By the end, they looked stunned trout."

"My grandma taught me to play poker when I was seven years old. She was deadly. No mercy. She'd even take money off priests and nuns."

They were both laughing so hard now that the truck felt like it was rocking. Vivian leaned on Jake's shoulder and stomped the floor with one foot.

∞ • ∞

Her glow of victory was short-lived. Shivering in the evening cold, she stared at Aunt Vanessa's brown-and-white milk cow, and knew she'd met her match.

Claire the cow looked huge and sinister in the shadowy light of the bare bulb that swung over the milking stall.

"All right, darlin', come have a seat," Jake directed.

"Are you sure she won't kick at me again?" Vivian sat down gingerly—practically under Claire's shifting back feet. Jake put his hand over Vivian's and guided her fingers gently into place on one of the cow's teats. Claire snorted.

So did Vivian. "Ugh. It's like grabbing a limp hot dog."

"*Ssssh*. You gotta pull just right."

"You do it, and I'll just watch. I like to watch."

"Viv, don't wrap your fingers around it so hard. No wonder nothin's happenin'! Stroke it, just stroke it." He chuckled. "You're gonna have to buy that teat a drink if you scare it any worse . . ."

"Listen, dude, I *know* how to stroke a . . . nevermind."

"Let *me* stroke it for you, Jake," a drawling female voice said from the barn hall. Vivian and Jake looked up quickly. Claire kicked over the milking stool, and

Vivian bounced onto the sawdust-covered floor.

"Marleen!" Jake exclaimed. He pulled Vivian up with one hand then clasped the other one on the shoulder of a tall, robust, blonde who wore her extra pounds in all the right places. Vivian brushed herself off, eyeing the proprietary way Marleen eyed Jake.

Marleen's big, hot body was outlined by skin-tight jeans and a striped sweater under a man's hunting jacket. Her hair hung halfway down her back in a thick mane.

"You must be Vivian Costa," Marleen said.

"The one and only."

Jake cleared his throat. "Viv, this is Marleen Burcher. Marleen, meet Viv."

Marleen smiled at him. "I just dropped by to say hi. I left Donny in October, you know. The kids and I have moved in with Mom and Memaw temporarily. I'm back in college. Should finish up my nursing degree in a year or so."

"That's good to hear."

Marleen gazed down at Vivian. "I've known Jake all of his life. We dated in high school. You should see my picture of him in a tux at the senior prom. Hot stuff."

Vivian drew herself up to at least five-foot-five. "I've know Jake all of four weeks. But I feel like we've spent *years* together with this cow."

Marleen smirked.

"Marleen, why don't you show Vivian how to milk?" Jake said gallantly. "She's a little leery of Claire." Vivian shot him an amazed look. He had no comprehension of this competitive female situation.

"Nothin' to it," Marleen said cooly. She plopped down on the milk stool, slapped Claire's rump to let her know who was boss, and immediately coaxed long streams of frothy white milk into the bucket. Vivian squatted on her heels to watch, praying that Claire would kick the highlights out of Marleen's blonde 'do. But Claire contentedly munched the sweet feed in her trough. Traitorous bovine angel.

Tiger, Aunt Vanessa's gray tabby, crawled into Vivian's arms and meowed.

"Wanta see a neat trick?" Marleen asked suddenly. "You'll like this, Vivian. Here you go, Tiger."

She aimed a stream of milk at Tiger, and he expertly caught it in his mouth. He slurped and swallowed while Vivian held him delicately away from her. She was staring at the cat when the thick jet of milk moved. It trailed over the left side of Vivian's hair and hit her squarely between the eyes.

"Whoops! Ohmygawd. Vivian, I'm so sorry."

Vivian dropped the cat and dashed milk off her eyelashes. "The milk facials at this spa could use some re-thinking."

Jake knelt down beside Vivian and tried to help, but one of his hurrying fingers poked her in the eye.

Marleen stood up. "Well, Jake, I'll be runnin' along. Don't see me out. I can tell you've got your hands full. You always did have a soft spot for helpless women."

With that parting shot, she stomped off. Jake frowned while Vivian muttered obscenities in Italian and wiped her face on her sleeve. "Marleen's not the spiteful type," he murmured. "We broke up after graduation and she married Donny. We've had no history since. I don't understand what just happened here."

"The only females you understand have horns and an udder." Vivian stopped cleaning her face long enough to stand up. He stood, too, and she glowered at him. "She left Donny. She's on the make again. I'm crowding her action."

"Okay, but why get mad at *me*? I'm not encouraging her."

"I just got *served*, Coltrane. *Capiche*? That was a womanly throwdown and I *lost*. I'm not a farm girl, okay? I can't milk or do anything else farmy. And I'm seriously buffaloed by this freakin' cow. I admit it."

"Viv," he said quickly, his voice deep and soft. His arms went around her "I don't give a rap-crap whether or not you can milk a cow."

"You probably say that to all the teat-challenged girls."
"I just thought you'd like to learn about farm life."

"I got a real kick out of it," she said dryly.

He looked at her somberly, from under his eyebrows. She gazed up at him just as somberly. They started snickering at the same time. He bent his head to hers. She gasped as the tip of his tongue flicked her skin. He was licking the milk off her cheeks.

"You taste good," he murmured. Remarkable sensations began to drift down Vivian's body.

She leaned against him and slid her arms inside his open jacket, curving them around his waist. "If you still think it's a smart idea to get mixed up with a city slicker, kiss me."

He did, his tongue transferring its movements delectably. Many seconds later, when their mouths parted, his ragged breath touched her closed eyes. "We're good together, Viv, no matter whether we're here or in the middle of Atlanta.

She opened her eyes slowly. "I want to know more about you," she whispered. "All of you."

He nodded, and they rested their foreheads

together. Just then the mellow, sweet sound of a dinner bell reached them from its source on Aunt Vanessa's front porch.

Their arms around each other, they walked out of the barn and headed toward the cozy house nestled in the hills.

CR • SO

The fixtures in the small upstairs bathroom were old, but scrubbed clean. They included a claw-foot tub and a green, metal medicine cabinet. Faded green tiles covered the bath floor, and ancient, flowered wallpaper covered the walls. Jake and Vivian stood on either side of Aunt Vanessa and listed while she told them which faucet was hot water and which faucet was cold water. She went through a litany of instructions for opening the latch on the medicine cabinet in case they needed an aspirin.

Jake nodded and said "Yes, ma'am," repeatedly, and Vivian got caught up in the hypnotic sequence of it and started nodding and saying "Yes, ma'am," too. Aunt Vanessa divided a stack of towels and washcloths and put them on separate sides of the Formica-topped sink.

"Left is yours, Jake-honey, land right is Vivian's," she explained.

"Yes, ma'am," Jake said.

"Yes, ma'am," Vivian echoed.

The bathroom was centered between the two upstairs bedrooms and it had two doors, one to each room. Aunt Vanessa clasped her hands to her bosom and turned to Vivian with concerned eyes.

"You just lock Jake's door whenever you come in here," she told her. "And you won't have to worry about a thing."

"Yes, ma'am."

She turned to Jake. "And you lock Vivian's door when you come in here."

"Yes, ma'am," he said solemnly.

"Well." Aunt Vanessa hugged each of them. "Happy dreams, my little chickies."

She clasped her hand sin front of her chest again, and twisted to gaze at Jake.

"Good night, honey."

Jake's carefully obedient eyes flickered to Vivian's amused ones and back to Aunt Vanessa. It was clear that he was being ordered away. Aunt Vanessa wasn't leaving until he was properly in his room, with the door locked.

"Yes, ma'am," he said gruffly. "Good night, Vivian."

"Good night, Jake," she replied primly.

After he clicked his door shut, Aunt Vanessa guided Vivian into the other bedroom and locked the bathroom door for her.

"I hope you'll be warm and comfortable in here honey. I'll bring another space heater up if you want it."

The old rooms were medium chilly, but the four-poster bed was piled with enough quilts to keep an army warm. A ceramic lamp with cherubs on it provided soft, yellow light from a long-legged night table.

"I'll be just fine," Vivian assured her. *Lonely and horny*, she added to herself, *but just fine*.

After one more hug, Aunt Vanessa glided out the door that led to the hall and left Vivian alone with the *whoooo* of mountain wind sweeping under the eaves outside. She looked toward the bathroom door mournfully. Jake was only about two dozen feet away, in a bed similar to hers—alone.

Vivian sighed and retrieved a Georgia State sweatshirt from her overnight bag. She shivered out of everything but her white panties then put on the sweat shirt along with thick athletic socks on her cold feet. Her floor-length terry robe had never been so welcome. Vivian had just finished turning the soft collar all the way up around her throat when she head Jake's bathroom door open.

Her breath caught in her throat. She listened intently and heard what sounded like a tall man trying to tiptoe across an old floor. He knocked on her door. She tiptoed to open it, but even her light feet made audible noises. The door opened with all the subtle silence of fingernails on a blackboard. Vivian winced.

"Hi!"she whispered when the door was open enough to see him. She leaned against the doorjamb in weak admiration. Jake wore a snug longjohn top tucked into his gray sweat pants, which were soft and clingy. White socks covered his feet, too. He had more clean, honest sexual charisma than any man she'd ever known.

"I'm sorry to bother you," he whispered coyly. "I just wanted to write down that word you told Aunt Vanessa, before I forget it. That Italian word for milk."

"Oh." She could barely repress her smile. "*Latte*. L-a-t-t-e."

"Thanks." He bent over quickly, brushed her lips with a warm kiss and started backing toward his door. The floor was both a chaperone and birth control device. *Creak, creak, creak.* "Good night, Viv. We can't make a single move up here without Aunt Vanny overhearing. She knows it, too."

Vivian made a needy, whimpering sound and shut her door.

Ten minutes later, she pried it open again and slowly slid her feet along the bathroom floor. The floor said *ungh uh, ungh uh*, with every step. Immediately, she heard Jake's bed frame rattle, and then quick squeaks as he crossed the room. His door inched open, and he looked at her distraughtly.

"I'm sorry, I'm sorry," she murmured. "Oh, I'm so silly. I just wanted to know if the rooster will crow in the morning. *Ssssh.* Forget it. Good night." |

She turned away, her head down.

Jake's broad hand snaked through the space in the door and circled her forearm. He bit back his laughter. His blue eyes were dark with interest. He inched the door open, and they stared at each other, breathing hard. Then the pressure of his fingers began to draw her toward him. The floor reported every step. She slipped her arms around his neck, and his went around her lower back.

Their mouths met gently, open and giving. He groaned in pleasure and tightened his hands against the top of her hips, urging her to press closer, which she did without hesitation. The hardness she found against his stomach was no surprise. The floor protested again.

"How can we possibly . . . " she rasped.

"Somehow, someway," he said gruffly. "I'll carry you to my bed."

The room was dark except for a square of light from the open bathroom door. Jake placed her on the bed and stretched out beside her, his hand on her stomach as she drew his head down to hers for another long kiss.

Long minutes passed in which they lay perfectly

still, just kissing and touching, their hands running over and then under the clothing that separated them. Her robe was now undone. Jake's fingers slid between the sweat shirt and her warm skin then began a tantalizing journey upward.

"You're quiverin'," he said, his lips against her ear.

"I want to move, Jake. You make me want to move, and I can't."

As if a reminder, the bed's box springs squealed. Jake's callused fingertips reached her breasts and rose slowly over them, an inch at a time, barely touching her but igniting tendrils of pure desire at every point of contact.

His thumb scrubbed languidly over a nipple. Vivian moaned and arched her back. He legs stretched out toes pointed, and kicked the footboard.

The whole bed shook, and the headboard whacked the wall.

"Jake," she whispered. "This is torture. And not in a good way." He nodded against her shoulder, withdrew his hand, and drew her quickly, impatiently against him so they both lay on their sides. The bed shuddered and thumped the wall again. Breathing hard, he buried his face in her hair, and she eased one leg over his hips.

Five seconds later they heard Aunt Vanessa coming up the stairs.

"What do we do now?" Vivian begged. "She'll hear me if I try to go back." "Stay here."

A delicate knock sounded at Jake's door. He looked down at Vivian one last, plaintive time, ran his hand down her body in good-bye, and climbed off the bed.

"Yes, ma'am? He called gruffly. He pushed the suspicious-looking bathroom door shut and padded to the hall door. Then he opened it a few inches and did his best to look as if he'd been asleep.

"Honey, would you go check the attic for me? Aunt Vanessa said anxiously. "There's so much noise up there that I think that family of raccoons must be back. If they don't quiet down, I'm gonna get my shotgun to 'em."

Vivian stuffed the edge of a quilt in her mouth.

"I'll sure do it, right now," Jake told her solemnly. "You go back to bed. I'll chase those critters out of there."

"Do you think Vivian's scared from all the strange noises?"

"No, ma'am. She was real tired, and I 'spect she's sound asleep."

"Good. Night-night, honey."

"Night-night," Jake replied drolly. He shut the door. He crossed back to the bed, took her hand, and sat down. "Sleep here, darlin'. I'll just get in your bed. It'll be quieter that way."

"What are you going to do now?" she asked with concern.

He sighed.

"I reckon I'm gonna put my coat on and go bump around the attic for a while," he said sadly.

"I'll miss you," she whispered. Jake arranged the rumpled covers over her and tucked her in. They kissed wistfully.

"I'll use the time to think about you," he promised. Vivian strained her eyes to watch him until he went out the door.

Then she grabbed an old wind-up alarm clock off the nightstand beside the bed and set it to ring at five a.m. With a plan brewing in her restless thoughts, she burrowed under the covers and waited for morning.

Chapter Eight

Jake and Aunt Vanessa sat at the kitchen table and sipped their second cups of coffee as if they'd been awake for hours, instead of just thirty minutes.

"Ooooh, I hate it when I oversleep," Aunt Vanessa complained.

They heard the clumping sound of footsteps on the side porch off the kitchen. Jake walked to the door and swung it open.

"What the . . . Viv?"

"Good morning," she said with a tired smile, her breath rising in clouds against the cold morning darkness. She had bits of sawdust in her dark hair and a stain on her coat in the shape of a cloven cow hoof. She handed him a stainless steel bucket full of Claire's bubbly milk. "I did it."

Aunt Vanessa came over and stared at the bucket along with Jake.

"Miss Vivian, I didn't know you could milk a cow! 'Specially my cantankerous old Claire!"

"We had a talk. I made her an offer she couldn't refuse." Vivian pulled a handful of sugar packets from her coat pocket. "I tried to fake her out with Splenda, but she only went for the full monty."

Jake lifted her off the floor, hugged her, kissed her lightly on the mouth, and whirled her around in a circle. "You'll be a farm wife yet."

"Put me down. You're churning my cream."

"Jake, you're embarrassin' her," Aunt Vanessa scolded.

Chuckling, he set her feet back on the yellow linoleum floor.

"Breakfast will be ready in thirty minutes, chickies," Aunt Vanessa piped. "Vivian, you'd best go get cleaned up. Jake-honey can you slice some bacon for your Aunt Vanny?"

"Yes, ma'am," he said dutifully. Vivian gave him a tentative, odd smile that he didn't understand. Jake's own smile faded a little.

"You feelin' all right, Tough Stuff? Did Claire kick you more than once?"

"She wouldn't dare. I'll be back in a few minutes."

"Farm wife," she murmured to herself as she went upstairs, wincing as one hand went to her back.

☉ • ☉

"Wake up, beautiful," Jake urged gently. She was curled against the truck's passenger door, her head pillowed on her folded tweed coat. The street lights of Atlanta flashed by her dozing profile. The night had turned colder, and rainy. "We're almost home. Another minute and we'll be at your place."

When she didn't respond, he patted her shoulder. She gave a soft cry of pain and arched away from his touch, fully awake in an instant. She looked at him with hazel eyes narrowed in a squint of discomfort.

"Viv, what is it?"

"Nothing. I just had a muscle cramp."

"What's wrong with your back?" he asked firmly.

"Okay, there's a spasm in my tail. I need to uncurl it for awhile. And the pointy red tip is sticking me in one hip. No problem. Just a Democrat thing."

He gestured toward her window. "My god, would

you look over *there*. I believe that's Alicia Keys comin'
out of the CNN building."

She pivoted toward the window. He knew she was
a fan.

Jake tugged the back of her sweater up.

Vivian had a long, ugly welt on her back.

She shoved her sweater down and glared at him.
"You punked me."

"Looks like Claire did the punkin'. She got you with
a horn?"

Vivian sank back on the seat. "Yes, but you should
see my teeth marks in Claire's ear."

He frowned the rest of the way to her condo
building. Jake swung the truck to a stop by the curb in
front of the high rise and clicked off the engine. "Come
on, let's get you inside. I'll rub some liniment on you."

"Jake, I'm worried about us. You belong in Tuna
Creek. You'll go back there as soon as you can. It's a
sweet place, but I belong here instead."

He looked at her as if she'd just taken his whole
world apart. She avoided his eyes and began gathering
her things. He said gruffly, "There's got to be a way,
Viv."

"I can't see it, at the moment." Her voice broke.
"I'm afraid we're headed for a painful reality check. I
don't 'do' cows. You need a woman like Marleen, not
me."

"Nothin' worth havin' comes easy, darlin'."

"Let's back away from each other and take a deep
breath and think about where we're heading. That's all
I'm saying. Please?"

He followed her up the steps to the building's
entrance. She turned around and faced him, crying.
"The world is screwed up. I see that in my courtroom

every day. It's not safe to love anybody too much."
Jake caught her by the elbows. "You've got it wrong.
The only way to survive is by loving as much as you
can."

"I have so many ugly pictures stored inside me,"
she rasped, bracing her hands against his chest, pushing
him back. "So much I've seen . . . so much I've
heard . . . "

He pulled her toward him an inch at a time. "All
you have to do is look at *me*, Viv."

"I need . . . " she began, and wanted desperately to
add *you*. But she just cried harder. "I need . . . " He
cradled her face in one hand as he continued to bring
her to him. The touch of his hand broke her. "I need
you, Jake," she said at last. "I need you so much. Help
me."

And then she was snug in his arms, her face hidden
in the collar of his coat, her hands clutching his
shoulders. He held her as if he'd let no force on earth
pull her away, and he twisted his head so he could press
his cheek to her forehead.

Then he scooped her up in his arms and carried her
inside the building.

ᥭ • ᥉

As soon as they stepped inside her dark living
room, Vivian sneezed and her teeth began to chatter.
Jake carried her to her master bath. He set her down
before flicking the switch on the row of lights over the
vanity mirror. Diffused light filled the cozy, luxurious
bathroom, reflecting off the coral-and-cream décor to
give everything—the dark wood cabinets, the oversized
white tub, and the two of them—a pink glow.

"Where's the thermostat?" he asked quietly.

"In the hall," she murmured, hugging herself and

wincing.

He turned a faucet and sent hot water whooshing into the tub. Next he grabbed a bottle marked Lavender Luxury and dumped most of the contents in the water. Scented suds exploded in the churning water. "Ease in and cover your goodies with the bubbles," he ordered drolly. "I'll come back in a few minutes with something warm for you to drink."

She nodded stiffly. He dropped a kiss on her neck and left, his heavy coat rustling as he removed it. Vivian numbly shed her clothes. Her back throbbed. She crept into the frothing tub and sank to her chin under mounds of lavender bubbles.

"Damn, I can't see a thing under those bubbles," Jake said as he came into the bathroom. Vivian laughed wearily, the sound ending in a yip of pain. A current of silent communication flowed between unspoken questions, mingled with the wordless knowledge that this was good and natural, that they were fighting the world together, tonight.

He sat down behind her on the tub and rubbed the rough surface of a coffee mug against her bare arm. He rested his other hand—the fingers spread—between her shoulder blades.

"Take a couple of big sips of this," he ordered, holding the mug closer. "What the bath can't warm, this will. I found that bottle of bourbon you bought for me."

He was right. The stiff, hot drink hit her stomach like an invasion of mischievous elves carrying torches. They quickly mounted an attack on the tourniquets that held her nerves taut.

"Okay?" he inquired. Each of his fingers had begun rubbing perfect circles on her wet skin.

"*Va bene*," she whispered.

"Bah what?" His voice was as warm as the water, and as caressing.

"*Va bene*," she repeated. "It means 'that's fine.' *Grazie*. That means 'Thank you.'"

"*Grazie*," he echoed. Vivian took another mind-relaxing swallow of doctored coffee, and closed her eyes.

His hand deserted her back. Vivian looked over her shoulder to find him taking off his blue-plaid shirt and the underlying ribbed top. He caught her gaze and stopped, his arms up and most of his chest exposed.

"Go ahead," she said evenly. But when she looked away, staring down at the water, her heart rate had begun a steady acceleration.

He tossed the shirt and the long john top into a corner. She looked around again, her lips parted. Vivian's eyes flickered over the well-developed shoulders and the lean muscle stretched across his torso. His thick, reddish hair contained an attractive dusting of sun-bleached blond.

"Nice highlights," she said.

"All natural," he countered.

His hands closed slowly over the tops of her shoulders. He sat down on the tub's rim, behind her. His denimed knee gently brushed her bare arm.

He slid his hands into the water, down her back, goading every tight muscle to give in. It was bliss. Vivian felt wrapped in the protection of his hearty soul. She set the mug on the edge of the tub, locked her arms around her legs, and put her head on her knees.

"Prettiest woman I've ever seen," Jake said tenderly, sincerely, his tone as soothing as the water and his hands.

For nearly a half hour he massaged her naked back. Her pain dissolved. Vivian turned and looked up at him tenderly. Then, slowly, she stood. The foam and fluff of scented bubbles tantalized him, letting only small glimpses of her body peek through.

She held out her arms to him.

"Viv," he murmured happily. He pulled a towel off his shoulder and dried her, smoothing the bubbles away, revealing everything. Once again he lifted her in his arms. This time he carried her to her darkened bedroom and tucked her under the girly white eyelet and thick blue coverlet. Rain pattered on a nearby windowsill. Her eyelids drooped in delicious response. "I don't want to fall asleep," she whispered. "This is not the effect you were going for. And not the one you were getting, I promise."

He smiled gently. "Take a nap. I can wait."

As he bent over her, kissing her forehead, her nose, her eyelids, she fell soundly asleep.

ଓ • ଅ

Jake forced himself to give her more than an hour before he returned carrying a dinner tray. He stopped beside the queen-sized bed, enthralled. The soft pool of light from a tiny porcelain lamp on the oak nightstand made her skin glow like hot honey. She lay on her side, her silky black hair drying into soft waves. Her full lips were relaxed, slightly parted. Her black lashes were tiny fans against her cheeks. Holding his breath, he set the tray down beside the lamp. She sighed and turned onto her back, her shoulders bare above the coverlet.

"Viv," he called softly. Jake braced one arm on either side of her and bent over to brush her forehead with his lips. "Wake up, darlin'."

Her eyes fluttered open, dark and dreamy. They

caught his and hypnotized him so much that he wasn't aware that he responded with a rough, loving sound that came from deep in his chest. But she heard it, and her face filled with heart-stopping adoration. He saw now, in this vulnerable instant before she could hide again, that she loved him, as certainly as if she'd spoken the words.

"Dear God," he whispered hoarsely. "Thank you."

Her hands slipped to the top of the covers and slowly pushed them down, revealing her breasts and the pink mist of desire on her skin. She put her fingertips on either side of his face and urged him to come to her. Her hands trailed up and down his chest. While he watched, transfixed, she slipped out of bed and knelt by his feet. She removed his boots slowly, and when she finished, she ran her fingers over his bare ankles and feet.

He smiled between short breaths. Her hands slid up his legs to the waist of his jeans. His eyes never left her face as she unzipped the faded denim. He shifted and helped her push his jeans and white briefs to the floor. Vivian admired him openly.

"You're magnificent," she told him softly. "Everything about you."

It might have been hours, it might have been minutes. They lost themselves in the glory of quick, new explorations. He rolled her onto her stomach and used his tongue to salve the bruise across her back, murmuring soft, nearly incoherent words of sympathy as he did so. He lay on his back and let her touch him as he had touched her earlier. Before she stopped, he was shifting on the bed with pleasure, his hands wrapped in tight fists around the brass rails behind the pillows.

"No more," he ordered. "No more."

"More," she ordered huskily.

He took her in his arms and lovingly put her on her back. His gleaming eyes held hers in a tender rebuke.

"Together," he urged.

"Together, then," Vivian agreed.

The weight of his body made an exquisite addition to her sensations. Vivian moved under it, testing the feel of him, aching to know how he'd feel inside her.

She looked up into his flushed face and half-closed eyes and felt an even more overwhelming rush of tenderness.

"Jake," she whispered. He kissed her deeply, then covered her throat in little nibbling kisses as his hands reach under, raising her hips in preparation. Slowly he slid inside her.

She matched every move he made, her hands skimming over his body to find new points to stroke as he stroked her. This time would be quick; they both sensed that. When the final burst of pleasure began inside her, it traveled swiftly throughout her body and exploded around him. "Jake," she groaned. "*Cara mia.*"

"My heart," he answered hoarsely.

She cried out again, and he matched the sound. He poured himself into her as she twisted beneath him, smiling, her head thrown back.

Jake wound one hand into hers and kissed her deeply as their bodies relaxed. Putting an arm under her shoulders, he held her tightly to him. She grazed his sweaty neck with kisses and wrapped her legs tighter around his hips. His mouth brushed her ear.

"My darlin' Viv," he murmured. "Feel the love and goodness in the world. It's all around us, it's here now."

He raised his head slightly, and she gazed up into

his face.

"I see it," she whispered.

☙ • ❧

After a long and tender night in Jake's arms, the buzz of her clock at 7 a.m. was a stark eye-opened she didn't want. Vivian leaned off the bed and whacked the snooze button with her fist. Immediately, Jake's arms surrounded her from behind and pulled her back under the covers.

"Calm down now, Tough Stuff," he rumbled, his sexy, sleep-roughened voice vibrating against the back of her neck. "We'll have thousands of nights together. This was just the first."

Vivian sighed wistfully, hoping that it would be so. Her hips and back nestled into the curve of his body, and the arm he'd put over her tightened. His hand roamed gently over her until it found a comfortable resting spot beneath her navel.

"Go back to sleep," he urged. "I love you."

"I love you, too," she whispered into the pillow. For a second they lay in silence. When he spoke again, his tone was gruffly teasing.

"Pardon me, ma'am. My hearin's not so good in the mornin'. Could you repeat that?"

"I love you, too," she said louder, with a little twist of exasperation. He rubbed her stomach.

"It'll get easier to say as time goes by," he said dryly, and dozed off again.

Vivian gave in to the heat of his body and the bed, and went back to sleep. At 7:40 she awoke with the instinctive knowledge that she'd overslept. The clock confirmed it.

"I have to leave for court in thirty minutes!" she rasped as she leaped out of bed. He grumbled and grasped thin air trying to capture her, but too late.

When she got out of the shower ten minutes later, her bed was empty and she heard pans rattling in the kitchen. She padded into the kitchen in her slip and a dark blue pin-striped skirt. Wonderful smells filtered toward her.

"How about a bacon-and-fried-egg sandwich?" Jake asked from his spot by the stove. He wore only his jeans. She whistled. He turned around and whistled back. "You wake up lookin' a whole lot better than I do."

He held out his naked arms and grinned a sweet, sexy-sleepy grin. Vivian tiptoed over on the cold tile floor and snuggled into his arms gratefully. He kissed the top of her head.

"You goin' to feel better today, Judge Costa?"

"I'm going to feel wonderful."

A strip of bacon popped and sent grease onto his uncovered back. Yelping, he turned the stove off. The he grasped her by the waist, lifted her off the floor, and began marching out of the kitchen. She dug her fingers into his shoulders.

"I have to go to work, Jake!"

"You give me ten minutes, I'll give you somethin' to think about all day," he promised.

"*Ohhhh*," she breathed, as they returned to her bedroom.

Twenty minutes later, she finished winding her hair into a French braid and wobbled through her living room, still flushed and her knees shaky, her jacket hanging over one arm. Jake strode out behind her with his ribbed top and plaid shirt crookedly arranged, his shirt tail trailing over his jeans.

"Here's your breakfast," he said softly, handing her

a paper bag. He gave her hurried outfit a once-over, took her hand, and towed her onto the sun porch. Early morning light gave the plant-filled room an ethereal quality. Jake turned her to face him and began straightening the bow on her white blouse.

"It's nice to be looked after," she admitted, her eyes gleaming.

He stroked wisps of hair back from her forehead, then caught her face between his hands and greedily studied her. "Be at my place right after work. Ready to spend the night. Oops. Sorry. Not meaning to order you around, Your Honor. Call it a polite but really, really hopeful invitation, awright?"

She stood on tiptoe and kissed him. "Awright." She mimicked his drawl.

"Say it one more time. Please."

"What?"

"You know."

She grinned. "I love you, Jake."

"Now git," he said gruffly. "And practice sayin', 'I love you, Jake.' You still put too much worry in the words."

"Because we still have lots of issues to discuss . . . "

"You'll be late for court. And I've got an apartment building to renovate." He kissed her to stop the conversation.

She sighed. "You win. For now."

ᚲ • ᛞ

She found the bulky package wrapped in white paper and blue ribbon on her desk when she came back from the morning session. Callender trailed into the office behind her.

"Jake Coltrane, you sweet boy," Vivian said under her breath as she glanced at the small card tucked into the package's bow. To Cal, who looked at the mystery gift with envy, she added, "Aren't men wonderful? Isn't life wonderful?"

"No."

"Bad day?"

"Yes."

Cal stalked out and, shrugging, Vivian tore into the present. She peeled the paper back, took a hurried look through the contents, and burst into laughter.

Tom stuck his head in the door.

"What's wrong?"

"Why would anything be wrong?"

"I never heard you laugh before."

She held up a pair of cut-off jeans and a frilly white blouse. "My *Dukes of Hazard* farm-babe outfit."

"Your *what*?"

"Never mind." Still laughing, she put the clothes down and pulled two books from the package. "And I got these. Look, *Dairy Technology and Livestock Management* and *A Day at the Farm*, 'For ages eight to eleven.'"

She stacked them on top of the clothes then retrieved something else, something she cupped in her hand. Her laughter faded to a soft smile.

"What's that?" Tom demanded. "A corncob crack pipe?"

"No." When she showed no sign of telling him what she held so protectively in her palm, he exhaled in disgust and left. Her eyes gleaming, Vivian held the tiny perfectly whittled wooden rose up and admired it.

"I love you, Jake," she whispered. "And I'm going to find a way to make it work."

Chapter Nine

She finished with the afternoon docket by three-thirty and had just plopped down to study a legal tome at her cluttered desk when Roberto, escorted by Barney Washington, appeared at the office door.

"Vivvy, you gotta go see about Jake!"

Fear raced through her, and she leaped to her feet.

"What's wrong with him?"

Roberto's rough hands twisted his red sock cap into a wad.

"Oh, I wasn't supposed to tell, he's gonna be mad . . ."

"Roberto Marino, you tell me what you're not supposed to tell, right now!"

"Oh, Vivvy, he's gone!"

"*Where?*" "To Tuna Creek?" she asked immediately, paralyzed.

"About an hour east of here, I think he said. It's on CNN. A bunch of farmers got together and barricaded themselves around a guy's place to keep the sheriff from servin' an eviction notice. One of Jake's buddies called him to come help out. They've got machine guns and everything! They fired shots into the air!"

Vivian was already shucking her robe and reaching for her coat.

ᴔ • ᴕ

The low, rolling pastureland gave her a long-distance view of the Melrose farm as she approached it down a country two-lane. Vivian winced at the beehive of flashing lights and news vans bearing satellite dishes. She got within a few hundred yards before a local sheriff's deputy blocked the road. Vivian parked the Prius to one side, jerked her credentials from her purse and ran up to a officer.

Still, it took ten minutes of pleas before the deputy let her walk into the area. Reporters seemed to be everywhere, mingling with dozens of heavily armed officers, including SWAT teams. A few curious local citizens had sneaked onto the premises, and a minister was singing "Amazing Grace." Vivian angled her way through the crowd.

The farm was a small, homey place with several outbuildings and a handsome split-level house at the end of a graveled driveway. The entrenched farm owner had built a barricade of farm equipment reinforced by sandbags around the house. Vivian strained her eyes to pick Jake out from the dozens of men and women behind the makeshift defense. *These must be forty people back there*, she thought in amazement.

And many of them held rifles.

"You can't just walk up there!" a reporter called.

"Watch me," she muttered calmly.

A burly, bearded man in faded overalls peered over the sandbags at her. "Ma'am, what's your business?"

"Jake Coltrane," Vivian said coolly. "Tell him Vivian is here."

"Well, hold on, hold on, let me check."

He turned to a group nearby, gesturing and talking on cell phones. They peered at Vivian and nodded. The bearded man came back and held out a hand.

"Climb over. He's in the house, having a cup of tea and being interviewed by some news folks."

Vivian pressed through a crowd of people into a corner of the home's living room and watched a television reporter from one of the south Georgia stations talk to Jake and four other people. The room was bright with the harsh, white light that accompanied the video camera. Jake looked very satisfied to be at the center of the attention.

"What if this standoff leads to violence?" the reporter asked.

"No, nobody expects that," he assured her. "That's just not the point."

"But you believe public opinion is quietly on your side?"

"Absolutely. People all over this country are losing their jobs, their homes, their hope. The laws are set up to benefit the bankers and the rest of the big money types, not the small farmer, the small business person, the ordinary citizen. We hand over billions in taxpayer money to bail out big companies but no money to bail out the small guy. It may be how the law calls it but the law isn't always sacred."

Vivian shifted uneasily. The reporter turned to interview other farmers, and Vivian caught Jake's eye. She crooked a finger at him then worked her way out of the room, stopping in a paneled hallway lined with family portraits. *I'll quietly whisk Jake out of here. Then I'll kick him off his milk stool and jab him with my horns.*

"Viv!" He grabbed her around the waist. "I'm hauling you out of here. This isn't a safe place . . . "

"Then why are *you* here? Why didn't you tell me? Don't lecture me about danger when *you're* involved in an armed stand-off with the police."

"The local mayor is right over there. And two local preachers, and see that little gray-haired lady? President of the chamber of commerce. I don't think there's enough room in the jail to hold all of us for long."

She pulled out her cell phone. "I'll make a couple of calls and get you out of here without being arrested."

"Darlin', I can't leave. This is what's right. I barely saved my own land, and I *did* lose the dairy business on that land, and it took the help of a lot of people to make the bank cut me even a little slack. I owe it to other farmers to support them. The laws are against us."

"That may be true, but you're supposed to work to change the laws, not resort to anarchy."

"This isn't anarchy. It's real well organized. At any rate, I'm not leaving."

"Oh, yes you are. It's very easy." Her voice became extremely patient. "You just put one foot in front of the other, and put your hand in mine . . . "

"No, no. Everything's settled. We've got it all negotiated. We're fixin' to let the deputies cart us off peacefully. Better publicity that way."

The front door burst open, and a dozen sheriff's deputies, SWAT team members and state patrol officers calmly stepped inside.

"Time to go, folks!" their leader yelled. "You ladies follow Officer Jenkins here."

"Scoot on out the back door, Viv," Jake urged.

"Nobody's going to arrest *me*," she said with complete assurance. "I'm obviously just a visitor." Officer Jenkins came toward her. "How do, ma'am," he said somberly, and tipped his wide-brimmed trooper's hat. "Come along."

"But you can't . . . I'm not . . . " Vivian sputtered. "I'm a municipal court judge in Atlanta."

"Yeah, right. And I'm Judge Judy."

Her eyes flew to Jake.

He gazed down at her with grim regret. "I'm sorry. I'll see you later, when we make bail."

"Come on, folks, let's move it!" a deputy shouted.

Officer Jenkins guided Vivian toward the door. She backed along, staring numbly at Jake, who blew her a somber kiss.

ભ • ૭

FARMER GOT A REPRIEVE FROM THE BANK.

Jake came out of the back rooms at the small-town jail with a deputy behind him and a worried look on his face. Vivian leaned against a desk in the deserted reception area with her arms crossed and her expression set. The deputy nodded to her and went into the back again.

"I tried to pay your bail," she told Jake. "But I hear you're not ready to leave."

"We're waiting on the local bank to guarantee an extension on the farm's mortgage. Then I'll leave."

"All you have to do is come with me before I change my mind about giving you a ride home."

"Look, I know you're mad about being arrested . . . I'm so sorry about that . . . "

"Hell, yes, I'm mad at you!" She tossed her hands into the air. "You jeopardized my reputation. You jeopardized your own life. And you didn't confer with me before you headed here to *take* that risk. What kind of relationship do we have if you don't respect me enough to warn me or even ask my advice?"

"I am sorry. You're right. I didn't think it through. I just knew what I had to do, and I figured it'd be best for you not to know. I knew you'd try to talk me out of it. I didn't want you following me here."

"I was appointed to this judgeship to finish the term for a judge who retired. But it's an elected office, so next year I'll be campaigning to keep my position. Do you know how my arrest record is going to look to voters?"

"Maybe it will give you extra street cred."

"That's only useful if I want to become a rapper."

"You knew I fought to save my own farm."

"*Lawfully.*"

Vivian cupped her forehead in one hand. "Just come get in the car. We'll talk about this at home."

"No. I'm goin' back in the cell. I'll pay my own bail."

"Fine."

He turned on his heel, went to the door that separated the reception area from the cells, and pounded it with one fist. The deputy peeked out a tiny window and opened the door.

"What ya'll want?" he drawled.

"Back in!"

An electronic lock clanked. The door swung open. With one last glare at her, Jake stepped through.

The door shut between them.

Chapter Ten

Two days later Vivian's intercom chimed. She had not heard one word from Jake since the jail scene, and she ran to the door hoping he was downstairs in her condo's lobby. She pressed the button and sang out drolly, "If you're here to apologize, I accept."

"Let me think what I've done to make women unhappy recently," a smooth, cultured drawl answered. "Hmmm. All right. I apologize for that, and the other, and oh, all right, for that incident involving the crème brulee and the martini shaker. Also, I swear to you, I had no idea the tattoo wouldn't be flattering. And, let's see . . . about the dancer. I should never have believed there's a respectable ballet company named the Exotica Review. . . in the meantime, let me introduce myself. I'm Rylan, Jake's cousin."

Vivian stared at the intercom. "Is he all right? He's not hurt, or still in jail . . . "

"No, no. Sorry, didn't mean to worry you. Jake's healthy and out of the slammer. I flew in for the day, just to check on him. He's obviously miserable about what happened. I'd like to talk to you on his behalf."

Vivian dully invited Rylan upstairs. When he knocked at her condo's door she opened it to reveal a tall, handsome and well-dressed blond man. "Hello."

"I'm sure from what Jake's said to you that you pictured me in overalls."

"And chewing a wad of tobacco. Come in and tell

me why Jake deserves to be more miserable than I am."

He laughed as he sat down on the couch. "He said you're a hard sell. I can see that."

"You're prepared to dislike me, aren't you?" she asked frankly. "You came here to see what kind of cranky bee-atch Jake's gotten mixed up with."

"Actually, I've heard nothing but glowing stories about you. Even now, all Jake will say is that he wishes he hadn't upset you. That's a pretty mild remark for a man who drank most of a pint of Jack Daniels last night."

"He ambushes me. I'm never quite sure what to expect. And I occasionally overreact."

"He loves you. He never says that lightly. Do you love him?"

"Yes, I do. I've never met anyone else like him. I'm just not sure how we're going to build a future that reaches from here to Tuna Creek and back."

Rylan stood. "Well, that's settled then. I can quit worrying."

"Is that all you came here to ask?" she asked, surprised.

"Yes." He headed for her door.

"Wait. Tell me something I need to know about Jake. Something that will help."

Rylan opened the door then halted. Looking back at her, he smiled sadly. "He loves surprises."

And then he was gone, striding to the elevator. Vivian shut the door and began making plans.

ᘒ • ᘓ

Barefooted, Jake sat in his kitchen with a cup of coffee and nothing but pictures of long-dead Coltranes to keep him company. He hung his head over the cooling coffee.

Mooooo.

At first he thought he was losing his mind. Then he knew he hadn't—there was no mistaking the low *mooooo* of a cow outside. Jake covered the distance from the table to a living room window in a few long strides, pushed the uncooperative old wood up with a mighty shove, and leaned out between his faded green drapes.

"*Mooooo,*" a small, brown-and-white cow called again.

"*Moooo,*" Vivian echoed. She looked up at him plaintively, her hand holding a thick lead rope attached to the placid cow's halter. Vivian wore stiff new overalls over a plaid shirt. She shivered in the growing cold of evening. "I brought you the one present I knew you couldn't resist," she told him. "She's named after a beautiful and famous Italian lady."

Jake sagged against the window frame. "Who?" he called.

"The 'Moo-na Lisa.'"

They stared at each other for a long, suspenseful moment. Then he slammed the window down and disappeared.

Vivian's hopes curdled.

"Come on, cow," she whispered huskily, and began leading Moo-na Lisa toward the street. Suddenly she heard the rattle of the gate opening. Vivian whipped around and watched Jake loping towards her. A smile burst out of her, and she dropped Moo-na Lisa's rope.

He scooped her into his arms. "I'm so sorry about all of it."

"I wasn't thinking straight the other day, either." She drew in the air with one hand, searching for words. "I was afraid, all right? What if you'd been shot by some trigger-happy SWAT officer? But I *am* proud of you. Your passion, your integrity, your anarchistic attitudes . . . "

"*Mooooo*," their bovine chaperone put in.

"We gotta take care of Moo-na," he said. "She's a prize performer."

"Udderly charming," Vivian quipped.

In ten minutes, Moo-na Lisa was back inside her trailer with a paid driver taking her up to Jake's land in Tuna Creek. Jake and Vivian walked back to the apartment hand in hand. Silently, that simple touch a lifeline between them, they entered Jake's kitchen.

They kissed quickly, then slowly, then intimately, and Vivian circled his neck with her loving arms. He ran his hands under her, lifter her, and spread her legs so that she could wrap them around his waist. Jake smiled at her as he sat down in a kitchen chair.

"Can't you apologize quicker?" she demanded.

"I've got more pride than I've got sense sometimes," he admitted, weaving his fingers through her hair. Their lips met, sampled, enjoyed. "I just wanted you to be proud of me the other day. When you weren't, it nearly killed me."

"I was, I am," she said. Her breath shattered against the top of his head as he nestled his face in the scoop of her neck and hugged her tightly.

"Will you marry me, Viv?"

All the color drained out of her face. "Let's make love and talk later. I've missed you so much."

"I want to know the answer, Viv. Hit me with it."

"Where do you expect to be a year from now?"

"Back in Tuna Creek running a new dairy farm. As soon as I get this place fixed up and sell it."

"Where does that leave the two of us?"

"In Tuna Creek, on a new dairy farm."

"Haven't you heard anything I've said in the past?"

"There's plenty of law to practice in Tennessee."
He grinned a little. "I'll handle the teats, you handle the
torts." When she just stared at him his smile faded.
"What exactly are you sayin', Viv?"

"I don't know yet. Isn't it enough to be together,
now, without worrying about the future? We'll figure it
out later."

"So we won't talk about marriage?"

"Not yet."

"Love and marriage aren't separate things—not in
my mind."

"Then let's not talk about either one."

"Fine," he muttered.

She pushed herself off his lap. "Fine."

"You gonna stay here tonight?"

"Yes!"

She stomped down the hall to his dimly-lit
bedroom and began pulling off her clothes. He
followed her, then stood in the room with his hands on
his hips and one leg angled out, watching her strip to
her panties. Blushing under his unfriendly scrutiny,
Vivian pulled the colorful quilts down and slid between
the sheets, then turned her back to him.

A minute later, she heard his clothes and boots slap
the floor with angry force. Jake settled heavily beside
her in bed. His long, hairy leg brushed her short
smooth one—he was much too big to avoid in a
double bed. So they lay there with the light still on,
together but achingly apart, their reunion strained and
unhappy. Vivian hugged her pillow.

He prodded her shoulder with one finger. "If I
pretend to cry, will you turn over?"

"Nope. No mercy."

"What do I have to do to get you to turn over?"

"Ask me to."

"Turn over."

"That wasn't 'asking.' That was 'ordering.'"

"Would you please turn over, dammit?"

Slowly, she rolled to face him. "There. Happy?"

He grunted. "No. But I'll do."

They burrowed their heads together and kissed. She huddled under the covers, kissing a path down his body. His back arched.

Much later, they lay side by side in the dark, holding hands. Jake sighed. She could almost hear him thinking.

"Stalemate," she whispered. "Give it a rest, Coltrane."

"No," he said firmly. "I have to get things settled between us." He brought her hand to his mouth and kissed it. "I'm gonna stay here."

"It's out of the question. You've got to go back to Tuna Creek, even if that means we'll have a long-distance marriage. You'd be miserable caged up here in the city."

"No. You're the most important part of my life. I'm gonna stay in the city. I won't sell the apartments, I'll play landlord. I've never expected to get diddly squat for this place, anyhow. Roberto and the others can keep their apartments rent-free if they'll help with maintenance."

"No."

"Yep. So that's settled." He wrapped her in his arms.

She sighed and let him think the discussion was over.

Chapter Eleven

"Brother Gabriel, it is now March. You have been a very bad boy since I last saw you in January."

"Oh, no, Your Honor, I am no longer addicted to my animal passions. Kanye no longer speaks to me from store windows. I listen to a high deity now."

Vivian leaned across her desk and eyed the thin, acne-scarred, earnest little man from head to toe. He wore voluminous brown trousers and unlaced sneakers, a green overcoat buttoned to his chin, and a tweed cap that was one size to small on his rusty hair. He carried a dog-eared *People* magazine and an impenetrable shield of righteousness. One of the doors at the back of the courtroom swung open, and she glanced up as Jake eased in. He grinned at her, cut his eyes to make sure no one was looking, and blew her a kiss. Vivian let the corner of her mouth crook up as if she'd caught the kiss.

"Brother Gabriel," she said patiently, "I am pleased to see that you are no longer annoying ladies on the street."

"Hallelujah."

"Amen," she reinforced. "But you cannot trade that habit for street preaching—not when you preach to the passengers of our public transportation system."

"But they are spineless, sinful devils," he said somberly.

"That could very well be true. But you cannot call

them that. It makes them angry. It makes the court angry."

"But he angels are happy," he protested, waving his *People*. "Angelina Jolie." He pointed at her photo.

"Angelina doesn't ride MARTA." The courtroom spectators tittered, and Vivian rapped her gavel. She let her gaze filter up for a split second and saw Jake leaning against a back wall at about the same angle as the droopy state flag next to him. His face was red with restrained laughter.

She cleared her throat. "Brother Gabriel, I see here in this report from your doctor that you're showing up for regular appointments at the clinic and taking your meds."

"Yes, Your Honor. And I'm working at a thrift store. I sort shoes and clothes."

"I'm proud of you. But if you want to preach you'll need to do it somewhere besides inside the public buses. I'll write you a list of approved locations. All right?"

"I shall behave," he promised. He leaned forward conspiratorially and whispered out of the side of his mouth, "You have blossomed since we last talked." He opened his magazine and pointed at a photo. "I asked Alec Baldwin to give you a happy heart, and he did."

"Why, thank you, and give my thanks to Mr. Baldwin, too."

"I will."

She looked up at Jake. *Thanks*, Vivian repeated mentally, Jake winked, pointed in the general direction of her office, and eased back out the door. With a half-smile, she turned her attention to Brother Gabriel again.

He gave her a thumbs-up.

She rapped her gavel. "The court recognizes your sincerity and your efforts to reform, and releases you on your own recognizance."

"Praise be!" Brother Gabriel shouted.

She was still smiling when she walked into her office an hour later. She saw Jake's chicken-scrawl note under the keys to his pickup on her desk. A pensive expression erased the dimple beside her mouth as she read.

"Will get Prius washed. Pick you up at 7 in my best duds. Love, Jake."

"Are you and Jake still going out?" Cal asked from the doorway.

"Yeah. We're meeting Jake's cousin. Rylan. He's in town on business, and he's staying at the Four Seasons."

"You look worried."

"Jake's paying. It'll cost him a fortune."

"But he wants to impress you."

"Cal, he's got a little book where he's written down every penny I've ever spent on the apartments and every penny I've ever given to his tenants. He keeps telling me, 'This entry here will come back to you in a mink coat one day. That one there will be a pair of diamond earrings.'"

"Oh, Vivian, I think I love him, too."

Callender clasped her hands in front of her and looked sentimental. Her long eyelashes trembled. Vivian stifled a wry smile. "The truth is that you just don't want to make Jake feel shabby," Cal went on. "You two are so sweet together."

"Don't get started now, Callender. Don't boo-hoo on me . . ."

It was too late.

"I envy you so much," Cal whispered hoarsely, and disappeared out the door, sniffling.

As usual, Jake was punctual as the sunset. Vivian heard her front door open, smoothed her hands down her oyster-white blouse and simple gray skirt, made an air-kiss at herself in the bathroom mirror, and hurried to greet him with open arms.

"Come right on . . . in."

He gave her a slow, charming smile as he shut the door behind him.

"Jake," she said ardently. "Dude. Baby. Wow."

He walked gracefully past her, grinning.

"Turn around," she ordered breathlessly. "Slowly."

"Seen enough?" he grumbled good-naturedly. "I want a kiss."

"I'm not through ogling you yet."

He wore a black coat over camel-colored slacks. His feet were cased in new cowboy boots. A crisp dress shirt of palest blue provided back ground for a black tie with tiny, angled gold and white stripes. Shirt cuffs peeked perfectly from the edge of the jacket sleeves.

"You like it, lady?" he asked softly

"I love it. I think I'll pack my Taser tonight. I may have to zap a few delirious women."

He laughed and held out his hands. Vivian crossed the floor quickly and slippede into his arms. Jake smiled down at her, still as capable of stopping her heart as he was on the night they'd met two months ago. They kissed tenderly.

ლ • �

"I *told* you she'd melt if you wore a jacket and tie," Rylan whispered, leaning closed to Jake's ear over their elegant restaurant table.

"*Ssssh!*" Jake glanced up furtively. Vivian would be

back from the ladies' room any second. "You were right. She was bowled over." Jake tugged at the tie and grimaced.

Rylan smiled. "I know you hate it. But you made Vivian happy, and that's what counts."

"Yeah, and just wait'll I finish. That deal I just clinched is goin' to make her sit up and take notice."

Rylan's smile faded. "Cousin, did it ever occur to you that she might not want you to arrange her life for her?"

Jake shot him a disgruntled look. "I don't have your pretty way of sayin' things. I have to depend on actions. She'll like this surprise."

"No, *you're* the one who likes surprises. If she hears what you're planning from someone else and misunderstands . . . "

"It's all taken care of. She won't find out too soon." Jake leaned forward, propped his chin on one fist, and sighed happily. "Ry, you just don't know what it's like to have a woman like Viv. . . "

"Do I hear my name?" the object of their conversation wanted to know. Both men stood as she settled into a chair beside them.

"All I do is talk about you, you know that," Jake said innocently.

"Right." She gave his shoulder a teasing shove, and he smiled as if she'd kissed him. Vivian turned to Rylan. "How did you like the music?" The three of them glanced toward a pianist playing soft jazz riffs at a baby grand.

"I wish he'd surprise me with some hip hop," Rylan joked. He caught Jake's eyes and nodded almost imperceptibly toward Vivian. "Do you like surprises, Vivian?"

"Not at all," Vivian replied distractedly. "I like to know what to expect."

She slid a hand over Jake's as she lost herself in the music. She didn't see the brooding expression that lined his eyes or the warning look Rylan pressed on him.

ભ • ৯

"How much food are you gonna give me, Viv? It's only a few hours' drive from here to Nashville. I won't starve."

Vivian put the last paper sack in the front seat of Jake's ole red truck. Then she put her hands on her denimed hips and squinted tartly up at him in the Saturday sunshine.

"You won't take any more of my money. So take my ravioli," she ordered. "It'll keep for almost a week if you put it in Rylan's refrigerator."

"I'll only be gone till Tuesday." He grasped her by the waist and set her on the truck's hood, then kissed her. They nuzzled each other like two friendly horses.

Vivian hugged his neck, inhaling good soap and wood smoke. "Tell Rylan I said hello. Then you hurry back."

"Viv," he asked seriously. "Will you always love me?"

"What kind of question is that? Of course."

"Even if . . . what if I did somethin' you didn't understand at first?"

"You already do things I don't understand," she joked. "Like putting sweet pickle relish on peanut butter crackers."

"No, I mean . . . innocent 'til proved quilty, right?"

Her joking attitude faded, and concern dawned in her expression. "What are you trying to tell me, Jake?"

He retreated quickly. "I just want you to feel you can trust me about everything in the world. That's real important to me."

"I do trust you," she said, smiling again.

"Good." He lifted her off the hood and swung her around. When he stopped, he kissed her repeatedly before he set her down.

She nuzzled her head against his chest. Jake caressed her black hair and stared down the long street awaiting him. His face was grim.

ᴄ⋅ᴐ • ᴐ

Monday started with bad news. Cal walked calmly into Vivian's office during lunch and told her she'd just resigned.

"You *what?*" Vivian exclaimed. Cal pointed to the chair across from Vivian's desk. "Mind if I use the therapy seat one more time?"

"No, but . . . "

"Good." She lowered herself into its creaking vinyl and looked Vivian straight in the eye. "Paul has a new girl friend." Vivian grimaced in regret. "If you can call a wealthy, fifty-year-old married woman a girl friend."

"I can think of a lot of other terms. What now, sweetie?"

"Now I get a divorce and move back to San Diego. My sister is going to let me stay with her for a while."

Vivian wasn't unhappy to hear about the divorce, only that Callender was leaving. Another thought occurred to her. She broached it carefully. "Whatever you do, try to believe there's someone out there waiting to love you again. Someone who may love you better than you've ever been loved before."

"I . . . hope so. I guess. I don't know, anymore." Cal got up and hugged her. "I'll be in touch."

"You're leaving right now?"

"Taking a few vacation days while I pack. I'll see you later this week." Before Vivian could say anything else, Cal turned and strode out the door.

∞ • ∾

That afternoon a secretary slipped into the courtroom and placed a note on Vivian's desk. Vivian scanned it quickly and rapped her gavel.

"Ten-minute recess," she said bluntly, and rushed out.

Andy, Roberto, Ray, and Fayra were all crowded into her office when she got there, their faces pinched with worry. Andy cried softly.

"Tell me what it is," Vivian said softly. "If something's happened to Jake, don't sweeten the words."

"No, nothing like that!" Roberto gasped. His hand shaking, he produced a folded letter from his faded jacket and handed it to her. "But read this."

Vivian took the letter. She swayed. She read it twice and still didn't believe it. When she looked up at the others, her distraught expression matched theirs. "He wouldn't have sold the apartments without telling us," she said hoarsely. "This must be a mistake."

"I didn't mean to open Jake's private mail," Andy whimpered, as she fumbled her way to her desk and sat down. "It was from a real-estate company, and I thought it was about one of those vacation places. Jake said I could open those letters, 'cause they give things away and he knows I want a ticket to Disney World."

"Where are we goin' to go?" Ray asked her bitterly. "Jake promised us a place to live in return for all our work. You know we've worked hard—long hours, six, seven days a week. And all the time he couldn't pay much, but we didn't care, because we had a roof over our heads and plenty to eat and friends."

"Jake wouldn't do this to you," Vivian insisted. "He wouldn't do this to me."

"Call him," Fayra urged. "Call up to Nashville and let's ask him right now."

She tried his cell phone. He didn't answer. Next she called Rylan's office. There had to be a reason. Jake probably had a whole, cute, homespun little explanation that would have them all laughing. And Rylan would know.

But Rylan didn't know, because Rylan was in Canada, and had been in Canada for a week.

Vivian felt the blood draining from her face. Jake had lied to her about visiting his cousin.

As she stared wordlessly at her phone, Tom looked in the door. "You're needed back in court."

"I'm on my way," she said automatically, her heart thudding.

"What now, Vivian?" Fayra asked in a tiny voice.

"Now we wait for Jake to call, or to come home. And we don't worry, because we all trust him, right?"

They brightened, buoyed by her enthusiasm. She guided them out the door with more words of encouragement. Then, after they disappeared around a corner, Vivian went in the women's restroom and sobbed her heart out.

ʘ • €

"Dammit, dammit, open up."

Vivian heard her own voice asking the caller to leave a message while she frantically unlocked her condo's door. She rammed the key into place, shoved the door open—and the phone beeped goodbye. The caller left no message. Vivian slammed the door behind her with a mighty swing of her arm and cursed. She had tried Jake's cell phone twenty times with no luck.

For the rest of the night she listened in vain for the phone to ring again. She finally dozed, dreaming about Jake until she jerked awake, covered in sweat from just having seen him push Ray and Fayra and Roberto and Andy out an apartment window, one at a time—just before he tossed her out behind them.

Chapter Twelve

She didn't want to alarm Aunt Vanny, so that morning Vivian called the feed store in Tuna Creek. It was a long shot, but the only shot she had left.

Emma Burley answered.

Vivian asked her if she'd seen Jake.

"Why, yes, late yesterday. He just about bought me out. Ordered a huge delivery of cattle feed. I know he's proud to get some of the Coltrane milk stock back. He had to lease his cows out when his business went bust."

"Did he say where he's going to put these cows?"

"Nope. Just roared outta here on some kind of mission."

She wanted to cry. She wanted to throw something. She wanted to get her hands on Jacob Needham Coltrane and call him two dozen choice names. And then beg him to make her believe she hadn't been a fool for the past two months.

With only a few minutes to spare before court convened, Vivian wandered around the halls of the municipal building, looking at nothing, hearing nothing, absorbed in memories. A loud voice poured out of an office.

"And so this redneck just says to me, says, 'I'll be right back,' and leaves his freakin' truck and this huge contraption it's pulling right across about ten parking spaces. He's gonna be towed in about five minutes, and he don't even care."

"Man, you get all kinds around here," a chuckling voice commiserated.

"What?" Vivian asked breathlessly. She approached two punkish undercover cops who lounged against a wall. "Who? When?"

"Just now," one said. "This cracker pulled in and left his rig in the main lot."

"Reddish-blond hair, tall man, driving an old red pickup truck?" Vivian asked eagerly.

"You got it, Your Honor. He disappeared up the street like he was goin' to a party or something. Got a cab and zoom! He's gone. I already called Traffic to write him a ticket and get his crap carted away."

"No! This one is mine. A personal problem. Can you guys do me a favor?"

They grinned at each other, then at her.

ᘏ • ᘐ

It was hell to sit in court and wait. Vivian forced herself to pay attention to the case in front of her, though her eyes kept straying to the double doors at the back of the room. A half hour passed. Then an hour. Finally, her head splitting with tension, she made herself stop wondering when they'd bring Jake to her.

"Detective Griswald, look at this report," she told the slack-faced man who'd testified in the case they'd just completed. She and Tom and Griswald hunched over the corner of her desk. "This isn't how you spell 'indecent.' This looks like 'indigent.' The man owns two hamburger franchises, so I doubt he's indigent."

The doors banged open. Vivian looked up quickly. The undercover cops shoved Jake into her courtroom with his hands cuffed behind him.

"Vivian, is this some kinda joke?" Jake demanded loudly, as they pushed him down the aisle.

They jerked him to a stop in front of her desk, and Vivian fought to control a wince. This wasn't nearly as satisfying as she'd hoped it would be. Jake looked disheveled and upset and completely innocent. He was supposed to look guilty.

She stared down at him. "You parked illegally."

"This isn't funny, Viv."

"That's tellin' her!" a spectator shouted.

She brought the gavel down with a fierce *whap*. "You have a lot of explaining to do," she told Jake calmly.

"He ain't got an attorney!" a man dressed in glittering drag complained from a back row. "He don't have to say nothing!"

She looked down at Jake impatiently. "Do you want an attorney?"

"I just want a chance to explain."

For the first time, Vivian noticed how tired he looked, how lines scarred the corners of his eyes and imprinted his forehead. *And his hair,* she thought suddenly, *his hair looks as if he hasn't had time to brush it for two days.*

"Take those handcuffs off him," she said abruptly. The undercovers mumbled and shuffled their feet and unlatched Jake's hand with obvious regret. Vivian nodded to them. "Good-bye, gentlemen, and thank you."

They ambled over to the side benches to sit down for the rest of the show.

"Viv," Jake said beseechingly. "What do you think I've done?"

Vivian looked down at him with just as much torment. "We'll talk later, if you'd like. Take your load of cow feed and your cows and go . . . wherever it is you're going to go."

She had to get him out of her courtroom before she burst into un-judgelike tears. "Let's have the next case," Vivian ordered gruffly. She rearranged papers with deceptive calm.

"You think you can haul me up here, embarrass me, act like I'm lower than slime on a snake's belly and then kick me out?" Jake asked.

"Good day, Mr. Coltrane, the court has nothing else to say to you at this time."

"Well, I have somethin' else to say to the court!"

Vivian glanced to her right as a coterie of detectives, attorneys and uniformed officers tensed for a confrontation. They looked at her for guidance, and she settled them with a gesture of one hand.

"You have five minutes, Mr. Coltrane." She checked her wristwatch. "Starting now."

He pivoted on the heels of his work boots and strode over to face the grinning spectators. He braced his blue-jeaned legs and clasped his hands behind his back. "I'm not right sure what Her Honor is accusin' me of, but as best I can tell, she thinks I've done less than I promised her."

"You promised to keep the apartment building," Vivian said.

"How'd you find out I sold it?" he asked, twisting around to stare at her.

"That's not important. And you're here to answer questions, not ask them."

Jake faced the crowd again, his back squared and his voice somber. "Ladies and gentlemen, can you blame a man for wantin' to make some money?"

"No!" they all chorused back.

"Well, then." He straightened proudly. "When I

inherited a run-down old apartment house here in town from my Uncle Needham, I thought I'd be lucky to make beer money off it. But then I begin to hear how the places on my street are bein' bought up by folks who want to live close to the city—folks with more money than they got sense."

"You tell 'em, man!" a drunk-and-disorderly case shouted.

"And I said to myself, 'Maybe I can make some money after all.'" Jake paused to glance back over his shoulder at her. "'That maybe,'" Jake continued, "I could make a lot of money, enough money to buy nice things for my lady, enough money to give us a nice home. Now, there isn't enough money in the world to pay her back for all the happiness and hope she's brought into my life, but I thought it'd be a start." He held his hands out in supplication. "And a million dollars ain't chicken feed."

A wave of audible gasps crested in the audience.

"I wanted it all to be a surprise," Jake continued, now pacing back and forth with his head down thoughtfully. "I planned to start puttin' a new life together, and then present it to my lady. I didn't know 'til the other day whether the deal was set on the apartments. I didn't want her to be disappointed if it fell through. I tried my best to come up with somethin' that would make her happy."

"Why didn't you just tell me you're moving back to Tuna Creek?" Vivian asked numbly.

Jake stopped and looked at her silently, his face registering surprise. Then he raised his eyebrows, nodded pensively to himself, and turned to the informal jury without answering her.

"Ladies and gentlemen, I went to Tuna Creek to

get my cows back. And to lease out my land there." He swung around and faced Vivian, his arms open and hands palms up. "With the lease income and the money from selling the apartments, I can afford to buy a little farm just north of here." Jake looked at her closely. "If Her Honor thinks she wouldn't mind makin' the drive into Atlanta every day."

Vivian took a deep breath. "What about Roberto and the others?"

"They go where we go," Jake replied gently, "if they want to. There's plenty of work on a dairy farm, and I'll pay good wages. But if they want to stay here in the city, I'll help them find work and give them the money to get settled somewhere else. So what's your verdict, Viv?"

Blinking back tears, Vivian looked at him tenderly. "You're guilty of stealing my heart." Everyone in the courtroom groaned. She rapped her gavel. "I'm afraid I have to place you in the custody of this court. For life."

Cheers rose around them as Jake bounded around her desk to kiss her.

ભ • ৪৩

"Tilt your head back, girl."

Vivian had trouble complying. She lay on her stomach, and Jake lay beside her with one long, naked leg hooked over her. He gently guided her head off the pillow, curled his head just-so, and kissed her. When he finished, she kept her eyes closed and smiled at him.

"Those eyes better stay shut," he whispered firmly.

One of her black brows twitched in surprise, but she pressed her lids tightly together. He trailed something up the center of her curving throat, something that was small and square and smooth.

It tickled her chin, her lips, the tip of her nose.

"Look," he murmured.

A tiny, beautifully carved wooden box sat on his open palm. "How pretty! It must have taken you forever."

"I've been workin' on it since right after I met you."

"I love it." He set it in her cupped hands, and she turned it this way and that, admiring the workmanship.

He snorted. "Well, *open* it."

She slowly pushed the lid up. Inside was a diamond ring.

Vivian curled it and the box inside her hands, burrowed her fists to her chest, and mumbled raggedly into the pillow. "Mine. All mine. Mine."

"Yep, the ring is yours."

She lifted her head and gazed at him adoringly. "Forget the ring. You. Mine. All mine." She hesitated. "But the engagement ring's not shabby, either."

Laughing, he took her left hand and slid the ring into place.

"It's beautiful," she sighed. "*Bella.*"

"Viv, you're not lookin' at the ring, you're lookin' at *me.*"

"Hush up," she purred in a Tuna Creek drawl.

EPILOGUE

Spring was lovely in the countryside north of Atlanta, and a few azaleas remained in bloom even though May was nearly over. Huge oaks surrounded the big Coltrane farmhouse, their limbs reaching curious fingers to stroke the clapboard siding and the windows of the upstairs bedrooms.

Vivian smiled and propped her bare feet on the front porch rail. The late afternoon sun peered under the sloping roof of the porch and, finding her agreeable, caressed her until she went to sleep.

Thirty minutes later, Jake crossed the grassy yard, dirty and contentedly tired from a long day's work, whistling under his breath. Chester and Phoebe stopped at the edge of the porch behind him, their wet tongues tasting the air as they were trying to figure out why he just stood there smiling at her. They snuffled his hand, and he shushed them.

Hearing Andy call them from one of the cabins house hidden on the other side of a forested hill, they loped away. Andy, Fayra, Ray and Roberto had made the move to the farm comfortably.

Jake took his boots off and tiptoed up the porch steps. He bent over Vivian. "You're not getting' the beans snapped that way," he whispered in her ear. She stirred and brushed at him as if she were shooing a gnat. He smiled wickedly. "I'll let you be this time, 'cause it's Saturday, and you had a tough week at court." She made a small sound of half-awake thanks.

"I love you, Tough Stuff."

She grinned up at him sleepily. "Now, *that's* worth waking up to hear."

He brushed the end of her tilted nose with his knuckle. "I'll be back in a few minutes, cleaned up."

"Need help?" Vivian asked as he disappeared indoors. Far on the other side of the screen door, the phone rang. She frowned in mild dismay. "Your tired body has just gotten a reprieve from being ravished."

"Oh, but I'm a repeat offender," Jake told her, holding the door as she hurried past him. "I'll probably do somethin' that I deserve bein' ravished for later on."

"I hope so." She planted a moving kiss on his cheek then trotted toward the phone.

Another thirty minutes passed before she ambled back to the porch, where a temptingly washed Jake now sat in the big rocking chair next to hers. He mimicked her earlier position, his denim-clad legs out in front of him, his bare feet crossed on the porch rail, his hands splayed over the white cotton T-shirt that left nothing of his muscled torso to the imagination.

"That was Callender," Vivian told him excitedly. "She's doing a lot better. The divorce was final this week, and she just got a job with the San Diego municipal court. She sounded . . . not thrilled, but content."

"Contentment will do," Jake said.

Vivian settled beside him in the other rocker. For a moment they watched cows trail across the rolling green pasture in front of the house. The cows were gentle black and white Holsteins, and she was learning not to be afraid of them. Moo-na Lisa made a brown-and-white oddity in the herd.

Jake reached over, snaked his fingers around her

rocker's arm, and nonchalantly slid Vivian and forty pounds of chair closer to him.

"Why, Pa," she preened, "I didn't know you still cared."

"Yeah, Ma, I still think you're the prettiest heifer in the barn."

Vivian tugged his T-shirt out of his jeans, slipped a hand underneath and tickled his stomach. "You say that to all the cows."

"Hold on, now." Jake stood up and pulled her up with him, then trapped her hands against his chest. "With bad behavior like that, you'll never get parole."

"Good," she answered.

And kissed him.

Clementine and Morning Glory

Coming April 2010

Two Novellas About Carolina Childhoods by
New York Times bestselling authors
Sarah Addison Allen and Deborah Smith

Excerpt

MORNING GLORY

South Carolina
State Motto: Dum Spiro Spero
"While I breathe, I hope."
July, 1975

The damp heat of a Charleston July pushed against
the funeral home windows. Mosquitoes and gnats
pecked the polished panes, trying to get my attention.
Let us in. We're real, this is life, red-blooded meals have to be
shared.

No, no. Boule blood is blue. And sacred. No
Feeding Allowed.

No longer did old-fashioned hardware-wire screens
give the hoi polloi of the insect world a fighting chance
at sucking Boule veins. Instead, the windows were shut,
and air conditioning units hissed in their lower frames.
Modern Palmetto Staters thumbed their noses at sub-
tropical nature. We preferred to be cool, and unnatural.

The world was changing. I imagined our ghosts basking in the artificial chill beside me while peering out at the pink bougainvillea vines—sun-freckled old sons of Confederates patting the lapels of their final suits, dead Disco-age babies dozing in their Baptismal gowns, and my deceased mother, Susan Moon Boule, an Up State Nobody, young, smiling, pretty, seductive, and buried (per my lurid imagination) in a pair of late 1960's trash-red Go-Go boots and a daisy-appliqued mini-skirt with yellow fringe on the hem.

My mother's ghost was not welcome in the Boule world of the Charleston coast. Her spirit was invisible to me. All I had of her were old photos and Boule whispers. All I had of her, was *me*.

I and the ghost brigade huddled by the funeral home windows together, wishing we could escape from Gran Boule's somber services, even it meant sweating. Hell hath no fury like a low-country climate in the summertime, but misery had no match like waiting for answers from the living whom the dead had left in charge of my life.

"Sign in, Maudie," Aunt Clairemont ordered. Sweating despite the loud, cold whoosh of the window units, nearly gagging on the funeral home scent of mums and carnations, I followed instructions and aimed a gold fountain pen (chained to a white podium with gilt edges, as if someone might steal it) at Gran's gold-and-white visitor book, embossed with MAUDE OCTAVIA BOULE MEMORIAL on the leather cover. The fact that I'd lived with Gran Boule on her sand-and-pine estate out in Mt. Pleasant (the hinterlands) since I was six months' old did not exempt me from cataloging my fealty as if I were a stranger.

Maudie O. Boule, I wrote. It wasn't easy to be a *Maude* in 1975, even in Charleston, where quaint old family names bloomed like speckled tiger lilies on heirloom stalks. There was just me, Gran and Bea Arthur on TV.

Spooky. Maude O. Boule was eighty-six and dead. Every notable person in Charleston had wandered into the funeral home's ornate parlor to study Gran Boule laying in her glossy white coffin, her mottled face curved in an unnaturally peaceful expression. *She looks peaceful*, they said.

She looks dead, I thought.

I, the other Maudie O. Boule, was twelve and alive. Yet *no* one saw *me at all*. They seemed to think I'd fade away if they didn't look at me, like an embarrassing memory.

Please, Daddy, take me home to live with you and your family, now. Please. I'm your eldest daughter. Please.

I dotted my i with a jagged asterisk. I swirled my final e like the tail of a coiled, hissing, copperhead snake. *Pleasssse.*

If Daddy still didn't want me, I had no where else to go.

CR • ЯО

A high, unseemly breeze suddenly ruffled the air at Gran's graveside service. The tops of skinny pines shimmied against a stark blue sky; two massive magnolias on the edge of the vast green cemetery came to life, clapping the hard paddles of their leaves. In the distance, tankers and yachts puffed fumes into the salt air. The warm Atlantic ocean of the southeastern coasts, an elegant lover cuddling the hot-blooded Caribbean, whispered to us. *Please, lure you away, you say? Draw you into the depths?*

I shivered. Was something blowing in from the wrong side of Respectability? Rude thoughts, scandalous secrets, more miseries? This was ungracious weather for a genteel Boule funeral. I huddled inside the humid crowd of nearly three hundred people, stifled by their bodies, my shoulders hunched and heart on fire in fear of my undiscussed future. Daddy stood by the grave beside his elder brothers and sisters, dark-haired and youngish and impossibly handsome, the crisp lines of his black, pin-striped suit untouched by the summer heat. Behind him stood his beautiful, blonde second wife and my half-sisters, their straight blonde hair falling in short, bouncy shags. Dorothy Hamill ruled the world of hair.

I was relegated to the third row. I swayed inside the black rayon of my A-line skirt and black, matching jacket, selected for me off the rack at a local dressmaker's. My scalp itched up to heaven and back. The sun fried the fifty-yard-line of exposed scalp that divided my red hair into two severe half-brains, neither of them happy.

Gran Boule's housekeeper, Sass Mol, had manacled my exploding hair with a tortoise-shell clamp that dug its sharp teeth into the nape of my neck. Below that clamp, my hair poofed down my back like auburn cotton candy.

My head looked like a skinned rabbit with a tail the size of a basketball.

The minister frowned at the odd summer wind and raised his voice above the once more.

Lord, we pray that you will welcome your servant, Octavia Louisa Springer Boule, into your bosom, and we know you're carrying her up the stairway to your kingdom, and that you will soothe the grief of her family—her sons Jameson, Beuffort and Devan, her daughters Mercie, Clairmont, Foxtane and Jeritha, and her many grandchildren--Bebe, Jims, Dou, Karabe, Sausa Mae, Clara, Marculene, Bos, Tomasina, Zees, Willyam, Betts,

Crawford, Francis, Frankie, Franks and Franka, Tulane, Mayfair, Peaches . . . and Mowdee.

Mowdee?

I don't care, I thought. But I did. T*hat* was the torture of a childhood begun in soft-spoken scandal, as prim and yet as shocking, in 1975, as a pimple on an angel's cheek. To care about having my name pronounced correctly. About the sorority of intimate vowels.

"Sister Boule is with the Lord," the minister went on, dabbing his flushed brow as the noon sun made steep shadows under his pale brows. A sweaty woman lifted her double chins and began to sing. A man armed with a violin accompanied her.

Nearer My God To Thee floated out to the pines and the Spanish moss on operatic waves and curious gnats. God was probably at Folly Beach, in a lounge chair, drinking a rum and Coke.

Gran's pearl-white casket was covered in a blanket of white lilies and little Confederate flags. I imagined her inside the stifling, airless heat of its satin-quilted interior, her diabetic eyes open balefully under her teased gray bangs, her swollen, diamonded fingers working her crochet needles the way a spider works a tasty, dead moth. Her mortician-pink lips pursed. Her ghost-words flew up around me; sucking my spirit out of me just like always. *No one blames you for your beginnings, so long as you don't turn out like your mother.*

"Amen," the well-to-do crowd chorused in the soft, beautiful voices of the coastal gentry, my daddy's sophisticated baritone resonating in my ears like a call to worship.

The service is almost over. What happens to me next?

My eyeballs turned itchy with Scare. My lids were petrified. I stared at Gran's casket so hard my brain felt like fried moss on pebbles left in the sun, burnt-brown and shriveled.

"Sister Octavia is surely resting in Heaven now," the minister finished, closing his Bible. "She was the anchor of an era, and we shall never forget her."

My Gran—born at Boule Hall forty-five years after the Civil War—died in two months after the end of the Vietnam War. So now she was a trail marker on the path between hopeless wars?

"Let us pray one last time," the minister said. *Again.* He must know Gran deserved, or required, extra supplication.

Everyone bowed their heads. I just *knew* they were thinking of iced tea with gin and crushed mint leaves in it and creamy potato salad and cold ham sandwiches with crisp lettuce, and the craving for a cigarette or the cool dive into the country club's pool and watching the summer reruns on TV. But mostly they were thinking of the gin. Drinking, in the hot coastal realms of Charleston, was a kind of air conditioning.

I stared at Daddy's broad back. Was *he* thinking about *me*? Getting ready to turn around and hold out his arms and say, "I left you with your Gran all these years because I knew she was lonely and she needed you. But now Maudie, you're coming home with me, where you belong!"

"Amen," the preacher said, again.

Clods of sand were tossed into the open pit of Gran Boule's grave. Gran Boule would now be planted beneath the tall, Art Nouveau, angel-adorned granite spire of the wealthy Boules, not far from the dead-family encampment of her parents, Mary Taunton Groover and Major Alton Johnathan Spruell IV, Confederate States of America, and beside her dead babies Unnamed and Unnamed and Unnamed and

Precious, Aged Two Years, and her notorious husband, Francis Ball Boule.

My Granfather Frank Boule (thirty years dead by then) was one of the Boules related to Martha Ball Washington and her husband George. Grandpa Frank Boule's blue-blooded Boule legacy hadn't saved his red-blooded behind from stepping on a strategically strewn mat of rusty tacks on the porch of the shanty house lived in by the farm black foreman's pretty black wife, or the resulting tetanus infection that swelled Grandpa Frank Boule's right leg up like a red balloon, until, festering and leaking pus, it killed him.

Gran Boule, so the rumor went, had dabbed her dry eyes oh-so-politely with her crochet-edged handkerchiefs at his funeral. Now, three decades hence, she must go into the ground beside him and account for those rusty tacks. Surely her ghost would admit that the Boules had never been able to resist the sweetness of forbidden berries, which must explain how my father and now long-dead mother crossed the tracks of class and decorum, and came to be together for less than a year, twelve years ago.

"Maudy, you little ornery shit, toss a lily on yo' Gran's coffin," a crackled voice said. "She done took care of you all these years. You better off than you know. So toss it."

A black hand, each finger thick and lined, poked my shoulder like a cattle prod. I looked up at Sass Mol. She wore a flowered hat on her fuzzy Afro hair, a floppy, print dress, and a scowl of Biblical proportions. Secretly, under her dress, pinned to the bodice of her slip, was an embroidered oval portrait of Dr. Martin Luther King. I was the only white person who had seen Sass Mol in her secret political lingerie. I would not tell on her. She trusted me.

White people liked to make up stories about kindly black mentors who are always old and harmless; it made us feel righteous, feeling so sweet toward the *coloreds*, as most in my family still called them then, but the truth is, we liked thinking of black people as elderly, kindly, and concerned with securing God's best graces on us white people. Uncle Thomas and Mammy and all that.

Sass Mol didn't fit the image. One of her enormous breasts hung low in her rose-flowered bodice; the other was gone. Sass Mol was lopsided. A black woman in those times might survive breast cancer, sure, but no surgeon bothered to mend her appearance or dignity. Just one of many reasons that Sass Mol did not take any shit off my little white self.

She fluttered her Maybelline lips. "Toss it, you sorry-sad little piss ant." She'd learned to shut out all sorrows she couldn't fix. It was as if I hadn't grown up hugging her fervently, or playing Monopoly at Gran's kitchen table with her grandchildren; like I had never pledged eternal best-friendship with her favorite granddaughter, Emily Dool, who swore to become a doctor.

Now I beyond Sass Mol's meager ability to help me.

My stony green eyes never left her red-rimmed black ones. I threw a white lily bloom at my grandmother's casket like a grenade.

"Be angry all you want, Maudie O. Boule. Nobody cares. It's up to you to prove they's wrong about you."

"You *know* something," I croaked. "Sass Mol, please. Tell me what you *know*."

She looked away, her eyes blue-black and watery.

People turned quickly from the grave, stepping like kids pretending to be solemn, not, like me, suffering a racing heart and the endless torture of The Great Unanswered Question.

Daddy *had* to love me back. He'd always sent birthday and Christmas gifts, wrapped professionally but signed on the cards in his own hand. He had always sent Gran Boule money for my clothes and school things. Even though it was a full thirty miles between his townhouse in Charleston and Gran's elegant old Greek columned house at Boule Hall, he had paid the postage on gifts and checks. And occasionally, he'd even visited. I was his daughter, his *eldest* daughter, and that carried some weight.

But now he was turning away from me too, cleaving to his elegant older brothers, their wives, their children, putting his arm around Esterline, smiling down at my half-sisters, Tulane, Mayfair and Peaches, who tromped solemnly in their princess jumpers and black patent Mary Janes toward his shiny, super-waxed Buick under the pines by the cemetery lane. The Buick was one of his dealership cars, with air conditioning and power windows, top of the line.

"Daddy?" I called. He walked faster.

Tulane, six, looked back at me with her pink face in a mewl of sorrowful goodbye. But Mayfair and Peaches faced forward, marching next to their society-conscious mother in their empire knit dresses, their pink leather purses on their arms like portable bombs. They were snotty, like their mother.

But Tulane didn't yet understand that I was the result of a family scandal.

"Maudie, me meow," she mouthed. "Me mow, mow wow."

"Mow wow," I said back, my voice cracking.

Sass Mol gripped my shoulder. "You ain't going. Deal with it."

The sun beat down hot on my braided red head; I could feel my freckles burning with fear as I kept trying to push through the smelly, scented crowd. "I'm going home with Daddy now. Of course I am. Family raises family. Gran told everybody I'd never be sent to live with people who aren't kin. She made Daddy promise. She put it in her will."

"Maudie, dead is dead, and it's the living that make the rules."

Suddenly the wind rose fiercely. The pines danced. The magnolias applauded like crazy. The crowd halted their quick-step toward potato salad and air conditioning, sharing a gape-jawed stare.

A late-model Mustang, gold-tone with red racing stripes, rumbled up the cemetery lane. It's unmufflered tail pipe said *Blubba blubba blubba*, like an old dog cheerfully passing gas. A racing scoop on its hood sniffed the air like a tawny metal lion. This predator, with its tacky, bronze-gold paint and Indian war-paint stripes, slunk into our midst. Above the stripe that zipped across the driver's door was painted in large, red letters:

MOON TOMATOES
Taste The Magic

Something had blown in from another realm, indeed. A universe that celebrated moons and tomatoes; a universe that glorified the *blubba blubba* vulgarity of bodily functions.

My mother's universe. The planet of her baby sisters.

LaVergne, TN USA
11 April 2011
223731LV00001B/83/P